4M /4F

NOW YOU KNOW

First presented at the Hampstead Theatre, London, on 13th July 1995 with the following cast of characters:

Roy	Paul Gregory
Terry	Adam Faith
Shireen	Luna Rahman
Jacqui	Rosalind Ayres
Liz	Julia Ford
Kevin	Simon Startin
Kent	Dave Fishley
Hilary	Louise Lombard

Directed by Michael Blakemore
Designed by Hayden Griffin
Lighting by Mick Hughes
Sound by John Leonard

CHARACTERS

Roy
Terry
Shireen
Jacqui
Liz
Kevin
Kent
Hilary

The action takes place in the general office of a small political presure group

ACT I
  SCENE 1 Night
  SCENE 2 Day

ACT II
  SCENE 1 Night
  SCENE 2 Day

Time—the present

Other plays by Michael Frayn
published by Samuel French Ltd

Alphabetical Order
Benefactors
Clouds
Donkeys Years
Make and Break
Number One (*translated from the Jean Anouilh original*)
Noises Off

ACT I

The general office of a small political pressure group. Night

The accommodation has been improvised out of attics and old storage rooms, high up under the eaves. All the arrangements are cramped and makeshift

An outer door leads to the staircase down to the street. Beside it is a switchboard/reception desk, closed off by a sliding glass screen. Three inner doors open into a library lined with files, a smaller private office for the campaign director, and a corridor that gives access to the mailroom and to an unseen washroom

A window opens on to the rooftops outside. A second window in an internal wall gives a little daylight to the otherwise windowless mailroom. This internal window is double-glazed, to soundproof it against the noises of the copier and printer visible inside

When the CURTAIN rises Shireen is on the switch. She is in her early twenties, and Asian. Kevin and Kent are working inaudibly in the mailroom. Kevin is thirty, and disabled. Kent is nineteen, and black

At the desk in the general office sits Jacqui, in her forties, trying to work at a VDU. On the other side of the desk perches Roy in his mid-thirties, holding a document. Terry, who is in his late fifties, is walking up and down the room

Roy And if you send it to the papers ...
Terry Disclosing. Right.
Roy Or if you go on one of your television programmes and wave it about in front of the cameras ...
Terry Knowing or having reasonable cause to believe.
Roy Knowing or have reasonable cause to believe that it is protected against disclosure ...
Terry Only I don't know, do I. I haven't got no reasonable cause.
Roy (*showing the document*) "Home Office. Secret."

The phone buzzes. Shireen answers it inaudibly

Terry I'm ignorant. I can't read.

Roy Look, I should be in a meeting. You asked me to come round ...

Terry Yes, but someone in the Home Office has leaked this to us. They've leaked it to us because they want us to plaster it all over everything. So how do we do it, Roy?

Roy I'm giving you my professional opinion.

Terry I don't want your professional opinion how not to do it. I know how not to do it.

Shireen slides back her glass screen

Shireen Oh, Terry, it's someone, I couldn't catch his name, he's from the *Telegraph*, it's about the White Paper thing.

Terry (*to Shireen*) We're a campaign for freedom of information, we get our tame brief round, and all he can tell us is how to keep information locked up.

Shireen Oh, sorry.

Terry opens the main door, and shows the sign on it saying OPEN

Terry (*to Roy*) Why do you think I called this campaign OPEN? Cause that's what we are. Cause any little secrets that go missing can walk in here, have a cup of tea, and then walk out again. (*To Shireen*) What, *Daily Telegraph*? Put him on to Jacqui.

Jacqui Today's the newsletter! I haven't finished the newsletter! Not to mention the membership renewals!

Terry (*calling*) Liz!

Shireen Only it's getting on for seven.

Roy (*to Terry*) I don't know why we don't do this in your office ...

Liz comes out of the library. She is in her thirties

Terry No secrets here, Roy.

Roy Well, there is, as a matter of fact. (*He indicates the document*)

Terry Was. Isn't no longer. Not now we got our fingers on it. (*To Liz*) *Daily Telegraph*. White Paper. Tell them.

Liz Tell them what?

Terry Anything they want to know.

Liz goes back into the library

(*Calling*) Tell them we got a leak from the Home Office about the Hassam case.

Liz (*from the library, puzzled*) Tell the *Telegraph*?

Terry No, Liz. Don't tell no-one. Roy here says send them their memo back, don't tell a soul.

Shireen I'll put them through ... (*She closes her screen*)

Roy Look, Terry ... (*He strokes the crown of his head*)

Terry Here, put it on. (*He feels in a blue cloth bag lying on the desk in front of Roy*)

Roy What?

Terry Your hairpiece. (*He produces a barrister's wig*) Your brains'll get cold.

Roy Terry, all I'm saying is this ...

Terry I know what you're saying. You're saying "Official Secrets Act — two years in jail." You said it when we done the Ministry of Defence last year. You said it when we done the Department of Trade and Industry. Well, don't you two-years me, old son, cause I know what it means, two years, and it's worse than what you think.

Roy I know ...

Terry You *don't* know, old lad.

Roy ... that you have personal experience ...

Terry Right — theft, false pretences, and occasioning actual bodily harm.

Roy ... because it's in our press release. But what about the others?

Jacqui Don't worry about me, my loves. Just let me get on with what I'm doing. And if Terry says do it, then do it.

Roy But we have to examine the consequences ...

Jacqui No, do it, do it! Tell everyone!

Roy looks at his watch

Roy (*to Terry*) I wish we could talk about this in private ...

Jacqui We'll all go to prison! Wonderful! The whole staff! At least I shouldn't have to write yet another appeal for contributions. At least I shouldn't have to keep on at those boys ... What *are* they doing?

She bangs on the glass. Kent and Kevin resume work

Roy Shireen — did she open the envelope? Shireen!

Terry Don't worry about Shireen.

Shireen slides back her screen, smiling

Shireen It's nearly seven, Terry. My mum'll kill me.

Roy Did you open this envelope, Shireen?

Shireen Yes, well, anything that says just like the name of the campaign. (*She takes off her headset and emerges from the switch booth*) Because usually if it's something secret it says kind of "Terry Little", kind of "Private and Confidential".

Roy But you didn't read it.

Shireen Well, I saw "Home Office", then like "secret", and I thought, oh hallo ...

Roy So then you stopped reading.

Shireen Well, I just read like, you know.

Roy You stopped and you handed it to Terry.

Shireen Yes, only Terry started jumping up and down and shouting ...

Roy Never mind what anybody said. You opened the envelope, you saw the words "Home Office — secret", and you handed it over. Anyone comes here and asks you questions about it, just tell them that. All right?

Shireen (*smiling*) All right!

Terry Don't have to tell Shireen what to say.

Shireen (*laughing*) Don't worry. Doesn't bother me.

Roy It might bother you if the police came and asked you questions.

Shireen (*shrugging and smiling*) No, I don't mind. (*She looks at her watch*) Only Mum's going to be so mad ...

Terry Get your coat, Shireen.

Shireen I just like sit in there. I've got things to think about. I don't worry about what goes on out here.

She goes out along the corridor

Roy What about the boys?

He indicates Kevin and Kent, obliviously idling on the other side of the window

Haven't told them anything, have you?

Jacqui What, and stopped them doing my mailout? Look at them.

Kent picks his nose

Terry Kent's busy, anyway.

Jacqui They think we can't see them in there.

Terry With Kevin it's his balls that need scratching ... There he goes.

Jacqui They think they're invisible, I don't know why.

Terry That's what they all think.

Roy Until we find out what's going on, and you wave it about on television.

Shireen reappears from the corridor. She stands in front of the window to the mailroom, putting on her coat

Shireen Police? It sounds like someone's been murdered or something.
Terry Right. They have.
Roy We don't know.
Shireen Murdered? (*She waits, interested*)
Roy That's what I'm saying! We still don't know what happened!
Terry Roy, don't give me this legal stuff!
Roy (*picking up the document*) All we know from this is that we *don't* know!
Terry We know they was telling us lies!
Roy But we don't know what the truth is!
Terry We know he's dead!
Roy If we'd got the complete story I'd say all right, let's go public, let's take the consequences ...
Terry We know he was OK when those coppers put him in the patrol van! (*He shows the document*) We know he wasn't OK when they dragged him out of it!

Kevin appears from the corridor, followed by Kent

Kevin (*to Terry*) Three minutes past ... Three minutes past ...
Terry Three minutes past seven. I know. Off you go, then, you two.
Shireen This is Mr Hassam?
Terry Oh, now we've got her interested.

Kevin makes his way towards the door, followed by Kent, but is distracted by the letter on the desk in front of Roy

Kevin (*looking at the document*) I don't understand ...
Terry And we know that three hours later they look in his cell and he's mysteriously suffering from a slight case of death.
Roy Which may have been the result of a heart-attack.
Terry Right, or the first symptom of a cold coming on.
Kevin I don't ...
Kent (*to Kevin*) Come on! They don't want you nosing around.
Kevin I don't understand ...

Terry takes the document out of Kevin's hands

Terry Only now for some reason we got the riot shields out, we got petrol bombs flying all over the West Midlands, we got questions in the House — and we got *this*.

Kevin ... the logical force of their argument.

Terry No, right, *I* don't understand the logical force of their argument, neither, Kevin. But then I don't understand the logical force of stopping you and me knowing about it. I don't understand the logical force of letting the buggers get away with it.

Liz appears in the doorway of the library

Roy Liz? What do *you* think?

Jacqui My God, we're not going to start *voting* on it, are we?

Liz (*smiling*) Why not?

Jacqui Why not? Because we don't work like that, my pet!

Liz (*smiling*) Don't we?

Jacqui We never *have*, my sweet! We've never had debates, we've never taken votes.

Liz Perhaps we should have done.

Jacqui There's something absolutely subversive about you, Liz, my precious.

Liz I thought there was supposed to be something subversive about all of us.

Jacqui What do you mean?

Liz Nothing. What about Shireen? What does she think?

Shireen Oh, I don't mind! It doesn't worry me!

Jacqui (*to Liz*) You sit out there grinning away with your hair in your eyes. No-one knows *what* you're up to.

Terry (*to Jacqui*) Come on, love, don't start on Liz.

Liz What about the boys, then? What do they think?

Kevin You can trust me ...

Terry We know that, Kev.

Kevin You can trust me ...

Liz How about Kent?

Kent What?

Terry Instant look of being somewhere else, with witnesses to prove it.

Roy What do you think, Kent?

Terry I'll tell you what Kent thinks. Don't know. That's what Kent thinks.

Roy Kent?

Kent (*shrugging*) Don't know.

Terry Don't know, right. That's two in favour, two against, two don't knows ...

Kevin You can trust me ...

Terry Three in favour. Right.

Jacqui Stop! Stop! Stop all this! Look, my loves, I didn't drop everything and throw in my lot with Terry because I wanted to hold *debates*. I did it because I believed in him, and whatever he thought I thought — because I was ready to follow him to the ends of the earth!

Hilary enters unnoticed through the open door from the stairs. She is a quiet, serious woman of about thirty. She stops in the doorway at the sight of them all

Roy (*getting to his feet*) Yes, well, if this is some kind of religious order ...
Jacqui All right! Why not?
Roy And our friend here is some kind of Messiah ...
Jacqui At least we might get something decided, something done, something improved in the world!

They all become aware of Hilary's presence

Hilary I'm sorry.
Terry Come in.
Hilary I'll wait outside.
Terry Wait inside. Who do you want?
Hilary It doesn't matter. (*She begins to go out again*)

Liz appears in the doorway of the library

Terry Come back!
Hilary You're obviously busy ...
Terry Yes, so come and help us. Close the door ... (*To Roy*) Member of the public, right?
Roy (*stroking his head awkwardly*) Terry ...
Terry Come in off the street. Never seen her before. Just the job. (*To Hilary*) Know about Mr Hassam, do you, darling?

Hilary looks quickly at Roy, then back at Terry

Hilary (*guarded*) Mr Hassam?
Roy Hold on, Terry ...
Terry The one who's on TV. The one who's in all the papers.
Hilary Yes?
Terry Read this, then, my love. This is what you *don't* know about Mr Hassam. (*He hands her the document. To Roy*) Decision. Right? End of argument. I've done it. I've disclosed. Ring Special Branch.
Roy Yes. Well ....
Hilary (*to Roy, not looking at the document*) I'm sorry. I waited. But ...
Roy I know. I'm sorry. I was just coming. I didn't realize this thing was going to go on. (*He takes the document out of her hands, and holds it out to Terry*)
Terry Oh, I see! This is her! (*To Hilary*) You're the meeting. He kept saying "I'm supposed to be in a meeting." (*He takes the document*)

Roy Yes, well, we must be on our way.

Terry So at last we've met the famous lady-friend. Lovely. (*He takes her hand*) Heard all about you. Haven't we, Jacqui? Always going on about you, he is. One moment you're in Chambers together — next thing we know you're living together.

Hilary glances at Roy

Roy Terry ...

Terry Two barristers in one bed! God help us! So — who's prosecuting, who's defending?

Roy Terry ...

Terry Right, don't answer that. Just say hallo to Jacqui before you go, since she's the one who keeps us all solvent. God knows how.

Jacqui Hallo.

Terry (*to Hilary*) And this is Liz, before she melts away like an ice-cream in front of our eyes.

Liz Yes, we have actually ...

She melts back into the library, embarrassed

Terry Oh, you have. Lovely.

Kent edges out of the main door

And that's Kent, that was. What's he doing? Nothing. Where's he going?

Kent Nowhere.

Terry Nowhere. Go on, then, Kent.

Kent goes

Roy Anyway ...

Terry And Shireen on the switch. Hear that smile of hers down the other end of the line.

Shireen (*smiling*) Hallo.

Terry (*to Shireen*) Don't keep your mum waiting, then.

Shireen No, but I don't know why everyone's so excited about this Mr Hassam person. No-one got excited when my friend's uncle was murdered. No-one did anything when my sister's boyfriend got beaten up. It's just like ... funny.

Shireen goes out

Terry Very funny. Must be. She's still smiling about it.

Kevin You can trust me ...
Jacqui And Kevin.
Terry What can we say about you, Kev?
Kevin You can trust me ...
Terry Right. You can trust him. Off you go, then, Kevin.

Kevin indicates the document

Kevin ... not to be garrulous.
Terry That's a lovely thought, Kevin.

Kevin goes out

It takes him a long time to get off the ground, old Kev. But once he's up in the air ... up in the air he is, good and proper. That's us, then. Off you go. Come and see us again. Oh — me, I'm Terry.
Hilary I know.
Terry (*to Roy*) She knew. Seen me on the box.
Hilary No, it was at a party.
Terry Once seen never forgotten.
Hilary No.
Roy So, if I could just have my wig ...
Terry (*to Hilary*) You got one of these, have you? (*He puts it on her*)
Hilary (*taking it off*) No.
Terry No? No tea-cosy?
Hilary I'm not a barrister.
Terry (*baffled*) Not a barrister?

Hilary looks at Roy

Roy This isn't Fenella. I don't know why you assume it's Fenella. This is Hilary.
Terry Oh. Sorry about that. Hilary?
Hilary Yes.
Roy I did try to tell you.
Terry Hilary. Right. (*To Roy*) So you and Fenella ... ?
Roy We're fine. Only Fenella's in Bristol. She's doing a public inquiry.
Terry Oh. Right.
Roy Hilary and I arranged to meet for a drink.
Terry Oh, lovely.
Roy For heaven's sake.
Terry I need one of these things and all. (*He takes the wig back and puts it on back to front, so that it covers his eyes*)

Roy And if I could just have that ...

Terry gives him the wig

Terry Sorry, Roy. Nice to meet you, Hilary. No, you're not a barrister. One look at you and I know that.

He ushers them to the door

So what are you then, Hilary?
Hilary I'm a Civil Servant.

Terry laughs

Terry Right! You're a Civil Servant!
Roy (*to Hilary*) Come on ...
Hilary I know what you think of Civil Servants.
Terry No — laughing at him, not you. Consorting with the enemy!
Hilary That's what I mean.
Terry Only joking, Hilary. I've nothing against Civil Servants, believe me. All in favour of them. Just want to see a bit more of you all.
Roy (*to Terry, holding the door open for Hilary*) I'll bring my draft of the report in next week ...
Hilary (*to Terry*) Why?
Terry Why what?
Hilary Why do you want to see a bit more of us all?
Roy Oh, for heaven's sake ...
Terry No, I'll tell you, Because you're a bashful lot, Hilary. You done an awful lot of messing around in my life, and I never had the chance to talk to you about it.
Hilary Go on, then.
Terry What, and talk to you about it?
Hilary Yes. What have we done?
Roy (*to Hilary*) We are a little pushed for time ...
Terry (*to Hilary*) Well, first off, Hilary, my love, you nicked me for something I never done.
Roy Oh dear.
Jacqui (*to Hilary*) This is when he was a child! (*To Terry*) She wasn't even born, my sweet.
Terry The people you work with, Hilary. Your mates.
Roy Look, let's get one thing straight. (*He closes the door*) It doesn't help our cause in any way to be rude and aggressive to public servants in private.

Liz appears in the doorway of the library

Hilary No, I asked.

Terry Yes, she don't need you defending her, Roy. She can look after herself. Can't you, Hilary? She's just as clever as what you are, I know that, or she wouldn't have passed the exam. Sit down, Hilary.

Roy Terry, please!

Terry (*to Hilary*) Sit down.

Jacqui Terry, they've got to go!

Terry Sit down.

Hilary sits down

(*Without looking round*) And you, Liz. You're on the jury.

Liz vanishes back into the library

Roy Look ...

Terry sits down opposite Hilary

Terry (*looking at Hilary*) I am looking. You look, too. You might learn something. (*To Hilary*) Yes, and when my mum died you shipped me and my brothers off to homes. One of us this way, one of us that. I ended up in Staffordshire. Why can't I be with my brothers? Because. Never you mind. You just do as you're told. Two years I was in that place, Hilary, and you never told me why.

Roy No, well, since this all happened forty or fifty years ago ...

Terry Yes, all you done since *you* been around is listen in to my phone calls and steam open my letters.

Roy No-one's listened in to your phone calls! No-one's steamed open your letters!

Jacqui (*to Hilary*) Anyway, I don't suppose he means you personally.

Terry No, I'm not being *personal*. *I'm* not being personal, *you're* not being personal. Never anything personal. Not your department, the nosepokers, I know that. You're not in the Home Office. You're in the bit that helps old ladies across the road.

Hilary gazes at him. He gazes back

Liz reappears in the doorway to the library

Roy Right, you've made your point ...

Terry Bet your mum and dad are proud of you, Hilary. Nice people, are they? Nice little house, nice little garden? Not one of the nobs, are you, like old Roy. Didn't come all that easy for you, any more than what it did for me.

Went down the road to school every day, did you, Hilary? Never messed around with boys? Did all your homework? Passed all your exams? Went off to college? Phoned home every Sunday? Mum and Dad come up to see you get your degree?

She is still staring at him. He is gazing back at her

Roy (*to Hilary*) You don't *have* to sit here and listen politely.
Terry No, *has* to be civil, don't you, Hilary, if you're a Civil Servant. One more question, then, and I won't say another word. (*He shows her the document*) That poor Mr Hassam the Home Office have been looking for. How did he manage to beat himself to death without anyone even noticing he was doing it?
Roy (*decisively*) Come on.

He goes to the door. Hilary remains sitting, looking at Terry

Terry What — no comment? Very sensible. Know things I don't know. Lot you could say if only you chose, et cetera. Not your policy to comment on allegations of this nature.

She continues to look at him. He looks levelly back

Liz vanishes again

Roy Hilary ...
Terry A cat may look at a king.
Jacqui Only which of you is the cat and which of you is the king?

Hilary looks away. She gets up

Hilary I never had a father. I was brought up by my mother, and we didn't have a house, and we didn't have a garden.

Pause

Terry OK, Hilary. Fair enough. A very frank answer, even if it's not the answer to the question I asked. Lot franker and more informative than what you usually get from a Government department. (*He puts his hand on her arm*) I never had much of a father, me neither. He buggered off and left us when I was two.
Roy Anyway, I've given you my opinion. I imagine you'll do what you usually do, which is what you were going to do anyway. And I'll bring that report in.

Terry What report?
Roy Secrecy in the legal profession.
Terry Oh, right.

Roy and Hilary go out

Walked right into that one.
Jacqui I knew it wasn't Fenella.
Terry (*laughing*) He'll be the worst of the lot, old Roy, when they make him a minister. Secrets? He'll be taking the name off the front of the Ministry.
Jacqui He's only behaving the way most men do, my love.
Terry You got to laugh, though.
Jacqui Have you.
Terry What — me?
Jacqui I'm not saying anything.
Terry When have I ever?
Jacqui Never. Never.

Liz appears in the doorway, putting on her coat

Terry What — last summer?
Jacqui I haven't said a word.
Terry I know what you thought, but it wasn't so.
Jacqui No.
Liz Sorry.

She goes back into the library

Terry Come on, Liz, if you're coming.

Liz reappears uncertainly

Liz No, I'd forgotten something ...
Terry You don't have to keep bolting back into your hole, my love, like some little furry animal. We're talking about that girl that come to do work experience last summer, only it's not so, it's not so.

Liz goes to the main door, smiling

So that was another of your strange chums.
Liz Well, I met her once.
Terry Never said, though, did you?
Liz No ... well ...

Terry Just went back into your hole and left us all to fall on our faces.
Liz It was a bit ...
Terry Awkward.
Liz Yes.
Terry Same as you.

Liz smiles

Another smiler. You and Shireen. Funny lot, smilers. Never know what's going on round the back.
Liz (*smiling*) See you in the morning.

She departs

Terry Her. Shireen. The boys. You. Five little worlds we got in here. And all of them a bit of a mystery, when you come right down to it.
Jacqui Six.
Terry Six?
Jacqui Yourself.
Terry No mystery about me, my love. Anyway, what's wrong with a bit of mystery. Moderation in all things. (*He looks at the document*) But I give her the memo! I give it straight back to the Civil Service, just like Roy said!
Jacqui So what are you going to do with it?
Terry Put it away. (*He puts it on the desk*) Think about it. Maybe they'll send us some more. Don't add up much on its own.
Jacqui That's not what you told Roy.
Terry No, well, I come on a bit strong. *You* come on a bit strong, and all.
Jacqui Did I?

He stands behind her as she works, and massages her neck

Terry Give it a rest, love. After seven.
Jacqui There's still the accounts ...
Terry Tell you what, missis. I'll take you out and buy you dinner. Once-off, *ex gratia*, no precedents established.
Jacqui It's Tuesday. It's my mother.
Terry Oh, right. (*He stops massaging her neck, and takes off his jacket*)
Jacqui No reason why you shouldn't come with me, though, darling.
Terry Fellow got up at the Tory Party Conference couple of years ago, remember?

He carries the jacket into his private office, and reappears, taking off his tie

Described me as a dangerous extremist. Not so, my love. Only thing I'm extreme about is moderation.

Jacqui You could just come for half-an-hour.

Terry Moderation. OK?

He goes back into his office

Jacqui begins to fold up her files

Jacqui You are coming home on Friday, though?

Terry reappears with a clean shirt on a wire hanger. He hangs it up and takes off the shirt he is wearing

Terry Friday?

Jacqui It's Poops's half-term. I did tell you.

Terry Oh, right ... Roy's little mystery, though. If someone said what was she like I'd say a helping of rather brainy mashed potatoes. I mean, all there on the plate in front of you. No surprises. Always the same with these mysteries, isn't it. When you finally get to meet them there's no mystery about them.

Jacqui You know Poops is riding Pippy at the local hunt thing on Saturday.

Terry Your ex'll be there.

Jacqui I mean I'll be out all day — you can take Bicky and Scrumps for a walk.

Jacqui takes the dirty shirt into his office

Terry You got your own life out there, though, haven't you? You got your house, you got your friends. You got Poops and Pippy. You got the dogs.

Jacqui emerges from his office, holding socks and underwear

Jacqui In the filing cabinet ... (*She sniffs at them*) All mixed up with the clean.

Terry You got the cat. Got me, come to that. Saturdays and Sundays.

Jacqui Why don't you *give* it to me? (*She puts all the underwear into a bag*) And that sleeping-bag must be absolutely crawling by now ...

Terry No, but that'd be extremism.

Jacqui Being there in the week?

Terry Living out there. For me. The middle of things, that's my territory, my love. Down Westminster, up Soho, meet a few people, find out what's going on. Half a mile this way, half a mile that way. Moderation.

Jacqui I meant what I said, though.

Terry What, believing in me?

Jacqui That hasn't changed, my sweet.

Terry Ends of the earth?

Jacqui Of which this office is one, as far as I'm concerned. I wish you'd let me take that sleeping-bag.

Terry Saving it up for Christmas. (*He gives her a kiss*)

Jacqui I'll give your love to my mother.

Terry Night, then.

Jacqui Night.

Terry Know where I'm going tonight?

Jacqui No. And don't want to.

She departs

He kicks off his shoes

Terry Right, then, white tie and tails. (*He takes his trousers off, then notices the uncurtained window. Calling out into the night*) Keep looking, darling, there's no charge ... Open to the public twenty-four hours a day, that's us. (*He folds the trousers, and continues to talk to the outside world, or to himself*) Anything you want to know, just ask ... Is it me? Yes, it is. See someone and it looks like me — it's me, put money on it. Any more questions ... ? Go on, then. What's my greatest satisfaction in life? — The Campaign. Being Director of the Campaign — What's my greatest regret? — No kids. All right?

He takes the trousers into his office, then puts his head back

Open book, that's me.

He goes into the office, and emerges with a dark suit. He holds it up and inspects it as he talks

Put it another way — I got my story ready. That's from when I was so high. Walking down the street, feeling the handle on the odd car, just in case. Up zooms the law. "What are you up to, son ... ?"

He fetches a clothes brush from his office and brushes the suit

No good saying "Nothing", like old Kent, cause then it's: "Right, loitering with intent — you're nicked." So let's try this one: "Going down the Council office, my dad works there." Might be true, all they know — might be trouble. And sometimes ... (*he hangs up the suit*) ... off they zoom again.

He goes out again

The sound of taps being turned on

Hilary comes in through the main door. She looks round uncertainly

Terry, off, splashes water over his head, snorts, and gasps with satisfaction. Hilary frowns, and decides to wait

Terry comes back in, still in his underwear, vigorously towelling his face and head

(*Under the towel*) I haven't got many qualifications for running a political campaign. I'm an ignorant bastard. But I got one: I'm me, and everyone knows it. Anyone wants me they can usually find me. (*He takes the towel away from his face*)

Hilary I'm sorry. I thought you were talking to someone. I thought Roy might be ... We had a slight disagreement. I thought he might have ... Anyway ... (*She opens the door to go*)

Terry Sit down! Five minutes, he'll suss you're here.

Hilary Tell him I've gone home, will you, if he comes back?

Terry Or come out and have supper with me.

Hilary No, thank you.

Terry Suit yourself.

He puts on the clean shirt and hangs up the hanger. She stands in the doorway looking at him

What? Knees? Nice, aren't they?

Hilary It was a charity evening.

Terry What was a charity evening?

Hilary Where I saw you before. You were talking to a woman who happened to be a doctor.

Terry Was I?

Hilary You were telling her why you hated the medical profession.

Terry Good memory you got, Hilary.

Hilary I watched you, I watched you quite carefully. I watched her, too.

Terry Why, what was she doing?

Hilary She was putting her head on one side, and making a funny little face, and laughing.

Terry You're not laughing.

Hilary No. (*She looks round the room*)

Terry What — comic way to live? I'll tell you something, Hilary ... Only
I'll put my trousers on first. I don't know why, but I can't hold forth in my
underpants. (*He puts on his trousers*) Right, so listen, Hilary — and it's
taken me half-a-century to find this out: everyone lives in a comic way.
Everyone? *Everyone*. They all got some funny arrangement in their lives,
they all got some special little way they're allowed to be different from
everybody else, only no-one but them knows about it. The people you work
with, Hilary — they look normal? They come in on the train every day, they
got a wife and kids? Watch out, sweetheart, because that means they got
something going on somewhere that's a whole lot more comic than what
this is.

She sits down in Jacqui's chair. He sits opposite her, and gazes at her

Hilary Look ...
Terry I'm looking.
Hilary Yes, and that's another of your little tricks.
Terry What?
Hilary This.
Terry See into your soul, Hilary.

Hilary looks away

Funny, isn't it — nobody wants their soul seeing into.
Hilary I've seen you on the television, too. I've heard you on the radio. You
don't argue, you don't present a case — you simply put on a performance.
You make it sound as if you're just being the plain reasonable man. But
you're not — you're being completely unreasonable. You say a lot of
funny things, but you're not funny, you're very aggressive, and very
destructive. It makes me angry. I'm sorry to be so un-Civil-Service-like.

Terry goes and picks up the kettle

Terry So, what, cup of tea?
Hilary Yes, and that's typical of the way you argue!
Terry I'm not arguing, Hilary. I'm listening.

Pause

Also waiting.

He offers the kettle, she ignores it

Hilary Look ...

Terry Got it from Roy, didn't you? All this "Look". Then he has a feel round the back of his head, see whether he's got his rug on ... OK. No more interruptions, no answering back, no tea. (*He puts the kettle down*)

Hilary It's the same for us as for everybody else. We *all* have to be free to discuss things frankly in private. To say what we truly think without hurting people's feelings or destroying their reputations. To disagree with each other in private, and then to present a common front in public. I don't agree with all our decisions, of course I don't, and it would be ridiculous if I couldn't say so while they're being made. But it would be just as ridiculous if I then went round telling everyone I didn't agree with what we'd decided.

Pause

And even if you *did* manage to find out what went on you'd discover most of it was so dull you wouldn't interested. (*She picks up the document*) And when something goes wrong then we've got to have some privacy while we investigate, otherwise we'll never find out what happened. We've also got to avoid saying anything that might make the situation worse.

Terry Biscuit?

He offers her a packet. She takes no notice of it

Hilary As a matter of fact it's not very easy work. And you're right, some of it's quite distasteful. So's what dustmen do, and sewage workers. And yes, it's horrible not being able to talk to people about what you're doing. I suppose you're thinking, then why am I having a relationship with someone in your campaign? Well, I'm *not* having a relationship with him.

Terry offers the biscuits again

Terry Special slimming ones. Made of sawdust.

Hilary I don't even understand what that's supposed to mean — a relationship.

Terry Jacqui gets them from the health place.

Hilary He's just someone I happen to know.

He takes one himself and puts the packet down

Terry So how long's this been going on, Hilary, this non-relationship?

Hilary I don't want to talk about it.

Terry Fair enough. Not another word.

He sits down at the desk opposite her. She abstractedly takes a wafer from the packet, breaks it in half, but doesn't eat it

Hilary And yes, I *did* work hard at school, if you want to know, and things *weren't* easy — they were extremely difficult, because I had to do a job in the evenings, and another one at the weekends. And yes, I got a first, and yes, my mother's proud of me, and no, I'm not ashamed of it. (*She puts the two halves of wafer down on the desk*)

Terry Ever wonder about your dad, Hilary?

She takes another wafer out of the packet

Sorry. Another question. Slipped out.

Hilary I don't want to talk about that, either. I shouldn't have said anything about it. (*She breaks the wafer in half*) Anyway, I don't know anything about him. I don't know what his job was. I don't even know his name. My mother never talked about him. We didn't talk about things like that. (*She breaks the halves up into little pieces*)

Terry Nevada.

Hilary Sorry?

Terry What you put me in mind of. All very nice and quiet, but then underground there's a nuclear test going on.

She drops the pieces on the desk and takes another wafer

Hilary There was a lot that Mum and I never talked about, now I come to think of it. I suppose it was good training for my work. (*She smiles bleakly*)

Terry Oh, nice.

Hilary What?

Terry You smiled. Lovely. You're a lovely girl, Hilary.

Hilary I must go. (*She remains*)

Terry I'll tell you a funny thing, Hilary. Your mum's not the only one who's proud of you. *I'm* proud of you. All right, I come on a bit strong before. Always coming on a bit strong. So people tell me. Jealous, who knows? No clever kids of my own, you see, Hilary. No kids at all. And I wasn't very nice to my mum. Me and my brothers used to give her hell, she didn't know whether she was coming or going, I think it was us that killed her. So I'm very glad you was good to yours, and you worked hard, and you did well. You're a good person, Hilary. (*He wipes his eyes*) Don't worry. Don't mean all that much — it don't take a great deal to make me cry ... Only it makes me think the Civil Service can't be so bad after all if it's got people like you working for it. Anyway, here's what *I'm* after in life, Hilary: heaven. You know what it says about heaven in the Bible — it's built of

gold. You know that — everyone knows that. But what sort of gold? You
don't know, Hilary, do you. I'll tell you: gold like unto clear glass. That's
the bit they all forget. Gold like unto clear glass. Transparent gold. All the
walls of all the houses in heaven. A golden light in all the rooms. Nothing
hidden. Everything visible. All kinds of comic arrangements you can see
inside those rooms, Hilary. People living in their offices, with their suits on
coathooks and their clean shirts in the stationery cupboard.

The switchboard buzzer begins to buzz softly

People living half the week with their sister-in-law, and half the week with
the postman's grandmother.

She looks at the switch. He gets up and crosses to it

But all of it open for the world to see. So no-one thinks there's anything
comic about it. (*He takes out Shireen's headset*) And if that's the way it's
going to be in heaven, why wait? Why not try and make it like that here on
earth? (*Into the headset*) Hallo ... ?

She watches him

Oh, hallo, Roy ... Has she come back here ... ?

He turns to look at her. She looks away and resumes breaking the wafers up

No — why'd she come back here? ... Talking to myself. Who'd you think
I was talking to? ... OK, Roy, any sign of her, I'll tell her. ... (*He repeats
to Hilary what Roy is saying*) You've gone home, you'll ring her in the
morning. ... Right. ... (*He puts the headset back, and crosses to her. He
stands looking down at her*) Awful mess you're making with them biscuits,
Hilary.
Hilary Yes.

She stops, and dusts the crumbs off her fingers. He holds out his hands

What?
Terry Coat.

She stands up and unbuttons her overcoat

Slow, aren't I? Got its advantages, though.

He puts her overcoat aside. She leans back against the desk, watching his hands as he begins to unbutton her shirt

Everybody else in the world knows the answer to everything already — they always did — it's no surprise to them. Suddenly I tumble it as well — and it really hits me. (*He stops, looks at the uncurtained window, then crosses to the light-switches*) OK — we haven't got to heaven yet.

He turns out the main lights. Only a shaded desk-light remains

I'll tell you what I like about women, Hilary ... (*he resumes unbuttoning her shirt*) ... you never know what they're up to. (*He unbuttons his own shirt*) And I'll tell you what women like about me: they always do.

She turns out the desk-light

Black-out

SCENE 2

The same. Day

Shireen is on the switch, Kevin and Kent are in the mailroom, Kevin working, Kent gazing into space and picking his nose

Jacqui enters through the main door, in her overcoat

Jacqui *Thirteen* separate beggars between Waterloo and here this morning, which I think may be a record.

Liz looks out of the library. It's probably Liz that Jacqui is addressing

The 8.18 was cancelled ... Hallo, my sweet.

Liz smiles vaguely

All right, my pet?
Liz Fine.

She goes back into the library

Jacqui *Plus* a signals failure at Staines ...

Shireen slides back the screen on the switch

Shireen Oh, Jacqui, someone called for Terry, I think it was Steve
something. And those people in Birmingham, they said you'd know what
it was about. (*She hands over the morning post*) Terry's out having a bath.
Jacqui Oh, thank you, my pet. Wonderful. Lovely. And the doorway
downstairs, my precious ...
Shireen Oh, the doorway!
Jacqui Knee-deep in cardboard boxes again.
Shireen Sorry, Jacqui, I forgot.
Jacqui It's not that I *mind* those two girls sleeping in the doorway. There but
for the grace of God. What I cannot see for the life of me, though, is why
it should be muggins here who has to fold up their boxes for them *every*
morning.
Shireen I'll do it tomorrow, Jacqui. (*She closes her screen*)
Jacqui And who Steve something is, and what all this is about people in
Birmingham, I have naturally not the faintest notion.

She bangs on the window of the mailroom. Kevin and Kent look at her

Yes, I'm here! Yes, I'm smiling at you! Yes, I'm going to go on smiling
at you! Smile, smile, smile!

*Reluctantly Kent begins to work. Jacqui sits down at her desk, still watching
Kent*

And Kevin, of course, will shortly be retiring to the loo for half the morning
... It's like Poops getting Pippy started when he's in one of his bloody-
minded moods — sheer heels and willpower ...

Liz comes in from the library

Liz So what was decided?
Jacqui What about, my love?
Liz Our leak. (*She picks up the document from Jacqui's desk*)
Jacqui Oh, no! He didn't leave it lying on the desk? (*She takes it back*) This
is supposed to be secret! I know we're against it, but honestly!
Liz What are we doing with it, though?

Jacqui is examining the document with distaste

Jacqui Sitting on it, apparently. Rolling about on it. Look — it's all *crumpled*! What's been happening in here! Shireen! Shireen, my precious!

Shireen slides the screen back

Who's been at my desk? Look, everything — it's *all* crumpled!
Shireen Oh, no! (*She emerges from the switch*)
Jacqui The pencils — they're all everywhere ... ! That's not where the stapler lives ... Where's my address-book ... ? Someone's been ... *crashing about* all over the top of my desk ... !
Shireen Oh, Jacqui!
Jacqui And my slimbreads! There's only one left! Someone's eaten them!
Shireen Oh, no, not your slimbreads!
Liz No-one *ever* eats your slimbreads.
Jacqui As it happens I haven't had any breakfast this morning ...
Shireen Oh, Jacqui, I'll run out and get you some more!
Jacqui No, but it's the *principle* of the thing. I'm perfectly happy to share. All people have got to do is come and *ask* me. (*She stops. She has found broken pieces of slimming wafer among the files on her desk*)
Liz What?
Shireen All like little broken pieces! They've like ... snapped them all in half!
Jacqui This isn't even thoughtlessness. This is wanton destruction.
Shireen Oh, Jacqui, isn't that awful!

Liz laughs

Jacqui Yes, well, it may amuse you. But this I am not standing for.
Shireen Perhaps the boys ...

They turn to look at Kent and Kevin, who are watching them through the glass

Liz Oh, I don't think so. Not your slimbreads.

Kent and Kevin go back to work. Jacqui starts towards the corridor, still holding the empty packet

No, Jacqui! Please! Don't start on the boys ... !
Jacqui And of course at once you take their side!

She goes out

Liz I can't bear it when she's like this ...

Jacqui appears in the mailroom

Inaudibly she gestures at Kent and Kevin with the slimbread packet. Shireen gazes at the scene, absorbed. Liz looks, then looks away, not knowing what to do

Shireen My sister keeps going on at me. "You've got to get off that switch, Shireen!" she says, "you got to do audio!" "Oh," I go, "I quite like being on the switch." "Don't be silly, Shireen!" she goes. "You *don't* like it! It's boring, nothing ever happens!"

Kevin is clutching an old ex-army haversack to himself, shaking his head

Liz Oh, no, not his bag!
Shireen What's he got in that bag, anyway?
Liz I can't watch this! (*She goes agitatedly to the door of the library*)
Shireen She's really going for him.
Liz She *knows* he never lets anyone see in that bag! I don't know how you can stand there and watch!

Liz takes refuge in the library

Shireen (*absorbed*) It's like, you know, this person's being tortured, only you've got the sound turned down ...

Hilary enters through the main door, and stops. She is carrying a bulky brown envelope

Hilary Oh ... (*She stops uncertainly*)
Shireen (*smiling*) Oh, hallo!

Hilary hesitates

Come in! We're having all like dramas this morning. Jacqui's on the warpath!
Hilary I was just ... (*She looks round the room*)
Shireen He's not here. Roy? He's in court this morning.

Liz appears in the library doorway to see what's going on

The confrontation between Jacqui and Kevin has subsided into more general nagging

Hilary No ...
Shireen Oh, what — Terry?

Liz You want Terry?

Shireen He's just out having a bath.

Liz Hallo ...

Hilary Hallo.

Shireen Sit down!

Hilary No, well, I was only going to ... (*She looks uncertainly at the envelope*)

Shireen I'll give it to him. (*She takes it*) Oh — it's a Private and Confidential. Lovely. He always likes getting Private and Confidentials! And lots in it, too! (*She puts it on the counter of the switch*) I'll put it over there, look, with his other ones.

Liz This is for Terry? (*She picks up the envelope and looks at it, puzzled*)

Shireen He'll be like a kid with a birthday present, won't he, Liz?

Hilary It's not anything very interesting. It's just ... well ... bits and pieces ...

Shireen Oh, don't tell us, don't tell us! We're not supposed to know!

The phone buzzes. Shireen goes back into the switch and puts her headset back on

(*To Hilary*) Only watch out for Jacqui! Someone's messed up her desk — they've broken up all her like slim things! (*Into the headset*) Hallo, OPEN ... (*She closes the screen*)

Hilary looks at the desk. Liz sees her look. Hilary looks away. Liz looks at the desk, then at Hilary, then at the envelope, then at Hilary again

Liz It wasn't you that ... ?

Hilary What?

Liz Her desk.

Hilary looks at the desk, then looks away

Hilary I've got to go.

Liz I didn't mean that. I just meant ...

Hilary Could I have it? (*She holds out her hand for the envelope*)

Liz This? I thought ...?

Hilary I've changed my mind.

Pause

Liz Yes. All right. (*She hands Hilary the envelope*)

Jacqui enters

Jacqui He's got *something* hidden in that bag, I know that. And the *smell* in there ... (*She stops at the sight of Hilary. Coldly*) Roy? He's not here. He's never here in the day.
Hilary No ... no ...
Liz She was just going.
Jacqui He's in court. I imagine.
Hilary Yes, I think he is.
Liz She was just going!

Jacqui sees the envelope that Hilary is holding

Jacqui What's this?
Liz Oh ...
Jacqui For us?
Hilary No. Well ...
Jacqui (*taking it and looking at it*) For Terry ... For *Terry*? (*She looks at Hilary*)
Hilary It was just something ... It doesn't matter ...

She tries to take the envelope from Jacqui

Jacqui Wait a moment. "Private and Confidential"? For Terry?

She looks at Hilary. Liz looks anxiously from one to the other

Hilary Yes.
Jacqui Oh. Oh.
Hilary I'll bring it back another time.

She holds out her hand for the envelope. Jacqui's manner changes

Jacqui Sit down, my sweet.
Hilary I made a mistake ...
Jacqui I'm not going to open it..
Hilary I just want to check ...
Jacqui Sit down.
Hilary I think I may have put something in I didn't mean to ...
Jacqui We can all have a cup of coffee together while we wait for Terry. (*She fetches the kettle*)
Hilary Thank you, but I can't really ...

Jacqui draws out a chair for Hilary and waits

Liz (*to Jacqui*) I think if she wants it back ...

Jacqui hands Liz the kettle

Jacqui (*to Liz*) Just fill this, will you, my love?

Liz stands holding the kettle. Jacqui indicates the chair to Hilary

Here!
Hilary Well ... (*She sits reluctantly*)
Jacqui My desk. The nerve-centre of the entire operation! No, but in fact it
is, because Terry's always at work on it as well ... (*To Liz*) Kettle!

Liz remains

(*To Hilary*) I'd offer you one of my slimbreads, but someone — no-one
here, of course, oh no — some mysterious intruder — I haven't got to the
bottom of this yet ...
Liz It was me.

Jacqui looks at her

I think it was me.
Jacqui You?
Liz I forgot — I knocked them off the edge. And they broke, and I tried to
pick them up ...
Jacqui Liz ...
Liz And I may have leaned on things ...
Jacqui Just fill the kettle for us, will you?
Liz Oh ... (*She goes to the corridor door, then stops*) Only ...

Jacqui waits

Yes ...

Liz goes out

Jacqui Dear Liz is in one of her flittering and squittering moods. What she
means is that I'm being unkind to Kevin, but I *know* it was him, Shireen saw
him, and you *have* to treat them just as you would anybody else, that's the
absolute basic principle. (*She looks at the envelope, which she is still
holding*) "Private and Confidential ..."
Hilary Would you give it to me?

She stands and puts out her hand for the envelope. Jacqui goes on looking at it

Jacqui Have you shown this to Roy?
Hilary No.
Jacqui No, well, Roy's a wonderful man. I don't know about his private life, of course, that's nothing to do with me ... But he is a lawyer, he *is* cautious — naturally, he has to be.
Hilary (*holding out her hand*) Please.
Jacqui And you're absolutely right to show it to Terry first. Sit down! I'll tell you something about Terry while we're waiting. Something you may not have realized. Sit down ...

Hilary reluctantly sits

Liz comes back in with the kettle, and plugs it in

He's a good man. (*To Liz*) I'm telling her about Terry. (*To Hilary*) I know, you see, because we've been in this together from the very beginning. We started the Campaign together! It was a kind of miracle. I was at rock bottom — we both were. Me in the middle of this truly ghastly divorce — Terry absolutely on his beam-ends.

Liz watches them anxiously, uncertain whether to go or stay, whether to intervene or be silent

I'd just been at my solicitor's — I couldn't find a taxi — when suddenly the heavens opened. So there we were, sheltering in the doorway of this shop, both feeling sorry for ourselves — and we simply looked at each other — and that was it. We started to talk, and we went on talking for seven hours non-stop. My precious, it was the Sea of Galilee all over again. I said, "You've just found your first disciple ..." (*To Liz*) You're like one of those maddening insects that can't make up their minds whether to come or go! (*To Hilary*) Yes, and when we were starting the Campaign I wasn't only his disciple, I was all twelve apostles. One room, that's all we had then. Just the two of us, living on faith, waiting for it all to happen. (*To Liz*) Liz, my sweetheart, you're scattering Nescafé all over the floor! (*To Hilary*) No, he's a good man. In fact I'll tell you something in confidence — he's a great man ...

Liz clashes the coffee-mugs together

Liz, sit down and let me do it! You're going to break something in a moment!

Terry enters through the main door with a bath-towel round his neck

Terry Right, I've decided. Thought about it in the bath.

Shireen slides her screen back

Shireen Oh, Terry ...

She gives him his letters. He crosses to his own office, looking at them

Terry (*to Shireen*) Call my old chum at Special Branch. (*To everyone*) That
leak—what does it tell us? Nothing. So, all right, we'll be good Scouts and
give it back to them.
Shireen And there's another one, a big one. Where is it?
Jacqui (*holding it up*) I've got it.

    Terry goes into his office

Terry (*off, to everyone*) Only we'll get some of our pals in the press round
to watch us do it ...
Shireen (*to Terry*) And *she's* here!

    Terry emerges from his office without the towel, still looking at his letters

Terry (*to Shireen*) Special Branch, number's on the pad. Inspector What's-
his-name, prat with a moustache. *Who's* here?
Shireen Her!

Terry picks up the letter

Terry And who screwed this up ... ?

*He looks up and sees Hilary. A coffee-mug falls out of Liz's hands and
smashes*

Liz I'm sorry. I'm sorry.

    Liz vanishes into the library

Jacqui (*to Terry*) Hilary. Roy's friend.
Terry Right.
Jacqui She came last night.
Terry (*cautiously*) Hallo, Hilary.

Hilary smiles awkwardly. Jacqui is discreetly holding out the envelope to Terry

Jacqui We've been having a little talk about things.
Terry Oh, yes?
Jacqui About the Campaign.
Terry That's nice.
Jacqui About you.
Terry About me?
Hilary I'm late for something ...

She gets up. Jacqui puts a restraining hand on her arm

Jacqui But I've been persuading her to stay. Because I think you and she are going to want to have a little talk about things as well.
Terry (*taking in the envelope*) What?

Jacqui goes on holding it out, looking significantly at him

   Liz appears in the doorway of the library

   What's going on?

Jacqui continues to hold the package

   "Private and Confidential"? What's all this?

He looks from Jacqui to the others. Hilary looks away

   Liz vanishes

He opens the envelope and takes out a file. Inside the file is a stack of photocopied pages

Shireen (*to Hilary*) I told you!
Terry "Home Office, secret. Mr K Hassam ..."
Shireen Oh — window shut!

Shireen closes her screen. Terry looks at Jacqui again, then reads. Silence. Jacqui watches him significantly. Hilary gets to her feet again. Jacqui restrains her

   Liz appears in the doorway of the library

Jacqui Aren't you? Going to want to have a little talk?

Silence. Then Terry looks up

Terry Fellow I was in prison with won ten grand once at roulette. He said when they call the number, and you know it's yours, it's like as if time stops for a moment ... You've died. You've gone to heaven. I think they just called my number. (*He holds up the papers*) It's only the whole file! All the memos, all the briefings! Only the whole story, that's all, only the whole cover-up! Right, into battle! Shireen!

Shireen opens her screen

Get me Mike Edwards, BBC News! He's in a conference? — get him out of the conference! He's on a plane? — get him off the plane! No, hold on. Let's think this out ... Get Roy first!
Shireen He'll be in court, Terry!
Terry Get him out of court!

Shireen closes her screen

Even Roy's going to say "Let's go" on this one! We've got you this time, Hilary! Got you good and nailed. Right, let's get it copied before anything happens to it ... (*To Jacqui*) I'll do it myself. Get the boys out of here.

Jacqui goes out to the mailroom

The fairies bring it — the fairies might take it away again ...
Liz (*distressed*) Terry ... (*She makes anxious attempts to indicate Hilary*)
Terry What — Hilary? I know. (*He waves the file around in front of Hilary. To her*) I showed you the last one — I'm not showing you this one!
Liz No ... no ... !
Terry (*to Liz*) No, nor you. All of us banged up we won't have no organization left. (*To Hilary*) Just go back and tell your chums in Whitehall — this time we're going to fry them!

Kevin and Kent come in, propelled by Jacqui

Kevin What ... ?
Terry (*to Kevin*) Doughnuts!
Kevin Doughnuts?

Terry gives Kevin money

Terry Six doughnuts. (*He glances at Hilary*) Seven doughnuts. Special treat.
Help each other choose.
Kevin Why?
Terry Celebrating. Bit of luck. Few quid on a horse.

He bundles them out through the main door

Kevin But ...
Terry Only take your time. Look inside each doughnut, make sure it's got
a full load of jam.

Kevin and Kent go

(*Going towards the mailroom with a file; to Liz*) You — back to work.
Jacqui — likewise.

Liz goes back into the library

(*To Hilary*) You — sit there. Be with you in a moment. (*He turns to go out,
then stops*) Hold on ... Shireen!

Shireen opens her screen

Shireen They're just getting him, Terry!
Terry Who?
Shireen Roy!
Terry Right. Just tell me one thing, Shireen.
Shireen Yes?
Terry Where'd this one come from? This didn't come in the post.
Shireen She *brought* it! She *brought* it!
Terry She *brought* it? *Who* brought it? (*To Hilary*) *You* brought it? You're
not ... you're not in the Home Office?
Hilary No.
Terry No. Sorry. For one horrible moment ...
Hilary But yes, I did.

Pause

Liz emerges from the library

Bring it.

Pause

Terry Where'd you get it, Hilary?
Hilary I copied it. From the file.

Pause

Terry I thought you said ... ?
Hilary I'm not. Now. I *was*.
Terry In the Home Office?
Hilary Yes.
Terry Was in the Home Office till when, Hilary?
Hilary Till this morning.
Terry Till this morning?
Hilary I've left. I've resigned.
Liz Oh, no! (*She claps her hand over her mouth*)
Terry You've resigned? This morning?
Hilary About ... (*she looks at her watch*) ... twenty-five minutes ago. I sent a note up to the head of my section. Then I came here.

Terry gazes at her

Shireen She comes in, she says, "Where's Terry?" I say, "He's out having his bath."
Jacqui (*quietly*) She was going to take it away again, my sweet.
Shireen I go like, "Sit down. Wait for him."
Terry (*stunned*) Oh, Hilary! (*He sits down*)
Jacqui I *knew* what was inside as soon as I saw it.
Hilary I was lying awake all night. I just started to think about it. About what it must have been like when he begged the police to help him, and they launched into him as well, and he knew there was no-one in the world left to turn to ... It just suddenly came into my head, I don't know why. But then I don't know why I hadn't thought about it before.
Terry What are you doing to me?
Hilary I got up and walked round the streets. I've never done that before. I think it was about five o'clock. Everything looked somehow very clear and sharp, and completely ... unreal. I felt slightly feverish. And terribly *excited*. (*She picks up a piece of broken slimbread, and breaks it into smaller pieces as she talks*) I didn't know what I was going to do! I might have been going to do *anything*! It was like being fifteen again and feeling the summer on your skin and wanting to take all your clothes off. Or all the words you mustn't say. Did you ever have the feeling that there are all these forbidden words inside your head, and they're red-hot, and they're burning a hole through your skull? They're shouting aloud inside you, and any moment they're going to come bursting out. Suddenly, in the middle of the

maths lesson, or when you're having tea with your family. You're just going to find yourself saying them. Or you're standing on the platform in the Tube, and the train's coming, and you can feel the edge of the platform kind of pulling you, and you think, "The one thing I mustn't do — the last thing on earth I *want* to do ... How do I know I'm not going to do it?" There's you and there's all these things inside you that may be going to do themselves ... I walked all the way into the office — I haven't had any breakfast! Then I remembered we'd got the file you wanted. It just seemed such a perfect fit. You wanted it, and we'd got it. So I drew it out, and went to the copier on the floor below ... I thought about people opening the envelope. And the pages sliding out. And the look on people's faces ...

Terry Two years, Hilary ...

Hilary I suppose it's a rather surprising thing to have done, now I come to think about it. It's very surprising! It's the most surprising thing I've ever done in my life! The worst thing. The worst thing I could ever imagine myself doing.

Jacqui Oh, you poor love!

Hilary No — it was so easy! I just put each page in the copier, and closed the lid and pressed the button. And that's all there was to it!

Liz laughs. She puts her hands over her face

I suppose I'm making it all sound a bit mad, but it wasn't mad in the slightest — it was perfectly rational. I just suddenly felt I'd lived my entire life keeping something shut away inside me. Shut away so tight that I didn't even know quite what it was. It wasn't *me* that was mad, it was the world — because a world where half the things you know are things you mustn't say is a mad world. And a world where no-one remarks on the fact is madder still.

Terry Two years, though. Two years out of your life, and no life to go back to afterwards.

Hilary It's not because of anything *you* said. If that's what's worrying you. I just ... started to think about it.

Terry OK, never mind two years. What about your mum, though — what would your mum say if she knew you was taking things from the people you work for?

Hilary Yes ... (*She looks out of the window*)

Terry I know you haven't got a dad ...

Hilary (*sharply*) No, and I don't want one.

Terry No, and I'm not dressing up as one.

Hilary Anyway, they're not people I work for. Not now. That's all over. I went back to my desk and wrote a note to Mr Hollis. I just said I was sorry, but I couldn't do the job any more ... He was a kind man, he liked me, he was bringing me on in the department ... But it's very simple. We all know what happened. Why not say it?

Pause

Terry Right. So here's what you do, Hilary. (*He puts the file back in its original envelope*) You put all this in one of them black plastic rubbish bags down the street. Not in our doorway, cause who knows? Someone else's. All right? (*He pushes the envelope across the desk to her*) Then you go back to the office. You tell that nice boss of yours you been under a lot of strain, you need a break, would he please tear up the letter. Then you take a couple of weeks' holiday, you thank Christ there's still one or two complete fools around in this world, and you get on and work your way up to Permanent Under Secretary. And if you ever get the feeling coming over you again, you just bung us a small contribution to the funds instead. Always much appreciated.

Hilary looks at him, and smiles

Then when you *are* Permanent Under Secretary, come back to us, and I won't give you no second chances.

Hilary gets up

Hilary Thank you. Jacqui's right. You're a good man.
Terry Straight back, then, Hilary. No funny turns, no am-I-aren't-I shall-I-shan't-I. So Shireen puts her headset back, excitement's over. Liz goes back into the library and finds us another good scandal instead out of the trade papers and journals, like she done before.

Shireen closes her screen

Liz Lovely, though. While it lasted.

She goes back into the library

Terry So *what* you going to do, Hilary? Just tell me. Just make sure we got it all straight in our minds.

She pushes the envelope back to him

Hilary I'm going to the Job Centre.

She goes out

Terry What have I done, Jacqui? What have I done?

Jacqui jumps up, and picks up the envelope

Jacqui I'll catch her on the stairs. (*She goes to the main door*) Because she
  could be, couldn't she?
Terry Could be what?
Jacqui Ours. Our daughter. If things had been different.
Terry Wouldn't have been more than six, my love, if so.
Jacqui No, but sooner or later she might have met some man. Thrown her
  life away. Because that's what this is all about, you realize. She's besotted!
Terry Is she?
Jacqui Oh, one look at her! And Roy's such a rotten devil!

Jacqui goes out with the envelope

(*Calling*) Hilary ... !

*Terry turns to go into his office, then notices the slimbread that Hilary was
breaking up*

Liz emerges from the library

*He starts to brush the pieces into the waste-paper basket, then realizes that
Liz has appeared. He indicates the desk*

Terry Bit of clearing up. OK? Because I don't like to think what you been
  up to here, Liz.
Liz (*laughing*) No ... I suppose that's why she came up and introduced herself
  to me.
Terry What?
Liz At that charity evening. I suppose that's why she made me introduce her
  to Roy.
Terry What are you talking about, Liz?
Liz Because we knew you.
Terry What do you mean?
Liz Nothing. Anyway, it doesn't matter, it's all over — you gave it all back
  to her ...

Jacqui enters, holding the envelope. She throws it down on the desk

Terry What, didn't catch her?

Jacqui Caught her. She wouldn't take it.

Terry So now what?

Jacqui I told her we'd find a job for her. (*She sits down at the desk and begins to work*)

Terry A job for her?

Shireen opens her screen

Shireen It's Roy! He's really cross! He was in the High Court! They've got him out!

Terry Yes, well, tell him ... Tell him to go back in again.

Shireen Oh, no! He'll go mad! (*She waits*)

Terry (*to Jacqui*) A job?

Liz What — *here*?

Jacqui Yes. Was that all right?

Terry No, it wasn't.

Jacqui Plenty of things she can do, my darling.

Liz Oh, no! Oh, Jacqui!

Jacqui (*to Liz*) For all of us ...

Terry Not all right at all.

Shireen (*into the headset, apprehensively*) Hallo, Roy, listen ... (*She closes her screen*)

Kent comes in through the main door, laughing, holding a cardboard tray of doughnuts

Jacqui What?

Kevin follows him anxiously, mopping ineffectually at his face and clothes with the backs of his hands

Kevin Jam ...

Kent Picks one up, looks inside, give it a squeeze ... out it comes, all over everything! (*He demonstrates — and covers himself in jam*)

CURTAIN

ACT II

The same. Night

Shireen is on the switch, Kevin and Kent are visible working in the mailroom.
Jacqui is sitting at her VDU. Hilary is sitting on the other side of the same
desk, trying to work. The door to the library is closed

Jacqui (*to Hilary*) Well, you know what Terry's like. He doesn't see what's
in front of his eyes. And it's not just the cardboard boxes. It's those soggy
paper plates with congealed food on them. And food isn't the only thing
they leave on those plates. I realize they've probably no access to toilet
facilities, but the plates they've been eating off — I mean, honestly! I'm
not madly fussy or house proud — we live in an absolute pigsty in
Sunningdale — the doorstep *is* how we present ourselves to the world.
Hilary I'll do it.
Jacqui Oh, my precious, certainly not. It's Shireen's job, but you know
Shireen — all she ever does is smile. Terry simply doesn't back me up on
this, it's hopeless. I try to keep the office running for him, but I can't do it
if people know he's not behind me.

Terry comes out of his inner office and stands looking at them

Go away! We're talking about you!
Terry It's six o'clock. It's knocking-off time.
Jacqui It's quarter to six. You go if you want to. We're enjoying ourselves.
Terry I thought today was the Newsletter?
Jacqui It is! I've done it!
Terry And the Hassam lobby? Definitely nothing we've forgotten?
Jacqui No! I told you!
Terry House of Commons? All our branches? All our tame MPs?
Jacqui Tell him, will you, Hilary? (*To Terry*) I know you don't trust *me*.
Hilary (*to Terry*) I think it's all covered.
Jacqui We did it together! Don't fuss! Go back in there! Shut the door if you
don't want to hear!
Terry Got to keep my ears open, my love. Check there aren't no plots or
conspiracies hatching out here. Make sure we're still all one big happy
family.

Terry goes back into his office, but leaves the door open

Jacqui He should be in Special Branch.
Terry (*off*) I heard that.
Jacqui (*to Hilary*) Anyway, you're still working. This is your Hassam thing?
Hilary It's just the background. So Terry can make sense of that file.
Jacqui He's not going to do anything with that file, you know, my sweet.
Hilary He's thinking about it, isn't he?
Jacqui For three days? I've never known Terry think about a thing for three minutes.

They both look towards the door of Terry's office

Jacqui Silence.

Pause

Hilary Tina and Donna.
Jacqui Sorry?
Hilary Their names. The girls who sleep in the doorway.
Jacqui Oh, you're so quick! Three days, and you know more about this place than I do!
Hilary No — I just happened to run into them.

Pause. Hilary works. Jacqui watches her

Jacqui Actually we'd quite happily chuck up Sunningdale and find some little place in Chelsea or Kensington, but Poops has got to have somewhere to keep Pippy, and we can't stable a pony in the middle of Sloane Square ... I feel bad enough about leaving the dogs all day, because I do think dogs have a right to a bit more out of life than two walks a day with a paid companion. Don't you?

Hilary works

I'm talking too much. It's funny — I don't usually get on with brainy types ... The house is far too big for us, though ... Is Roy keen on pets?
Hilary Roy? I've no idea.
Jacqui It must be a tiny bit intimidating, having rows with a lawyer. Or don't you have rows?
Hilary Not really.

Pause

Jacqui What does he think about your working here?
Hilary I don't think he knows.
Jacqui You haven't told him?
Hilary Not yet.
Jacqui You mean you haven't seen him?

Hilary stops trying to work

Hilary Well, it's all quite complicated.
Jacqui Fenella?
Hilary Among other things.
Jacqui Oh, my sweet love! But he hasn't even phoned?
Hilary I've been out a lot.
Jacqui Honestly! Men!
Hilary Well ... and women.
Jacqui I mean, I know what it's like, believe me. When there's someone you love, and you can't live with them ...

Terry comes out of his office

I'll tell you when it's six o clock!

Terry hesitates, then goes back into his office

Pause

Hilary (*suddenly*) Yes, and you want to talk about them all the time, and say their name, and tell everyone ...
Jacqui And you have to keep biting it back ...
Hilary And you think you'll die if you don't say it just once ...
Jacqui Because you have to be terribly discreet and sensible.
Hilary And you can't believe it's not written all over you, and shining out of you.
Jacqui Oh, my poor precious!

Pause

Hilary Perhaps we shouldn't be quite so discreet and sensible.
Jacqui No, perhaps not.

Pause

When did you meet those girls?

Hilary Tina and Donna?
Jacqui They're never around in the day.
Hilary No. No ...

Terry comes out of his office again

Terry I don't care what time it is. It's Friday evening, and we're all going
home. Come on, Shireen! (*He bangs on the mailroom window and
indicates his watch*)

Shireen slides her window back

Shireen What?
Terry It's the weekend!
Shireen Oh, lovely!
Terry So busy listening to these two rabbiting you never noticed.

Shireen emerges from the switch

Shireen I had my window shut! Honestly!

She goes out to the corridor

Terry What do you think, then, Hilary, end of your first working week?
Hilary It's very nice. Everyone's very friendly. I've enjoyed it.
Jacqui It's you, my sweet! You've transformed this office! Hasn't she,
Terry?
Terry Yes, when you think what it was like in here last week. Everyone
shouting and screaming. Can't even remember now what it was all about ...

Kevin comes in carrying his haversack, followed by Kent

Jacqui *I* can.
Terry Oh, yes.

Kevin struggles to get something out of the haversack

Kevin This is just something ... Just something ...
Kent Come on, get it out.
Kevin Just ...
Jacqui What — something for Hilary, is it, Kevin?
Hilary For me?
Kevin Just ...
Jacqui A bar of chocolate, yes, we can see.

Kevin Just something ...

Hilary Oh, Kevin, you mustn't spend your money on me.

Kevin Something ...

Terry So that's what he keeps in that bag of his. I've always wondered.

Kent laughs

Terry What?

Kent (*shrugging*) Just laughing.

Terry Anyway, that's a beautiful thought, Kevin.

Kevin Something ...

Hilary Thank you, Kevin. It's really sweet of you.

Shireen comes back from the corridor, putting her overcoat on

Jacqui (*to Shireen*) Kevin's bought a bar of chocolate for Hilary!

Shireen Ohhhh! Isn't that nice!

Kent tries to pull Kevin away

Kevin Something ...

Kent Come on, she don't want you hanging round all night.

Kevin Something ...

Shireen Lovely weekend, everybody! Lovely weekend, Hilary!

Hilary Yes. And you.

Terry Night, Shireen.

Shireen goes out

Kevin Something ...

Kent Don't mess her about, Kevvy!

Terry So what are you up to this weekend, Kent?

Kent Me? Nothing.

Terry Oh, that'll make a change.

Kevin ... to mitigate the shortcomings of the office coffee.

Terry Oh, it's to mitigate the shortcomings. That's why he can't get the words out — they're all a yard long.

Hilary Anyway, I'm very touched.

Jacqui Now just leave her to eat it in peace.

Terry Night, then, Kev. Take care.

Kent pushes Kevin out

Don't wobble off the platform on the way.

Kent (*to Hilary*) See you Monday.
Hilary Me? Yes. Good-night.

Kent goes out

Jacqui A bar of chocolate, though! I think you've made a tiny bit of a conquest there, my love.
Terry What about old Kent? "See you Monday, Hilary." I've never heard him making fancy speeches before. Saucy bugger.
Hilary (*looking at her chocolate*) It's books, usually.
Jacqui What?
Hilary In Kevin's bag. He goes out in the lunch-hour to buy them.
Jacqui Oh, there's quite a little thing going on between you two, isn't there, my sweet!
Terry Not careful we'll have Kevin and Kent murdering each other in there.

Terry goes back into his office

Hilary Well, if we really are all finishing ... (*She stands up and folds up her work*)
Jacqui I was just thinking ...

Pause. Hilary waits

What peculiar creatures men are ...
Hilary You mean ... Kevin?
Jacqui No ...

Pause

The library door opens, and Liz comes out. She sees Hilary, and stops, all smiles

Liz Oh, sorry.
Jacqui What?
Liz Nothing. I thought ... (*She goes back towards the library*)
Jacqui What *is* the matter, Liz, my sweetheart?
Liz Nothing ... nothing ...
Jacqui This is the umpteenth time you've done that today! You don't like the look of us?

Liz smiles and closes the library door

What with him popping out of there, and her popping out of here ... It's like living in a shop full of cuckoo clocks ... ! She always used to leave the door open — I don't know what's eating her ... Of course she lives with some woman friend of hers. I can guess what *that's* all about, not that it's anything to do with me ...

Pause

Hilary Peculiar creatures. Men. You were just saying.
Jacqui Oh, yes. Don't you think?
Hilary What — Terry?
Jacqui Terry?
Hilary I thought you might be thinking of Terry.
Jacqui Yes. Or Pippy.
Hilary Pippy?
Jacqui Poops's pony. Although I'm not sure he counts as a man because he's been *done* ...

Hilary laughs

Jacqui What?
Hilary What people tell you and what they don't.
Jacqui How do you mean?
Hilary Well ... No.
Jacqui What?
Hilary Nothing. Only you always say "we".
Jacqui Do I?
Hilary "We have this person who walks the dogs ... We're going to have the garden remade ... "
Jacqui Yes, well, Poops ...
Hilary Isn't she away at school?
Jacqui Half-term — I told you.

Pause

Hilary Yes. I'm sorry. Forgive me.
Jacqui Anyway, there's Pippy. And the dogs.
Hilary And the cat.
Jacqui Well, I *do* think of them all as "us" ...
Hilary Of course. I'm sorry. Anyway ... (*She goes to the corridor door*)
Jacqui You mean I'm always asking about you and Roy?
Hilary Oh ... No. Not at all.

Jacqui You never say "we".
Hilary Don't I? No ... "We ... us ..." (*She laughs*)
Jacqui What?
Hilary Strange words.

She goes out through the corridor door

Jacqui stands up and stretches, then opens the library door

Jacqui Do *borrow* her! (*She goes back to her desk and puts her things together to leave*)

Liz appears in the doorway

Well, you're being so funny about it! I don't want to monopolize her. I told Terry she could work for both of us. He wouldn't have taken her on otherwise. It was hard enough persuading him as it was.
Liz Jacqui ...
Jacqui Even though he *adores* her.
Liz Jacqui, I can't bear this!
Jacqui Why, what's the matter?
Liz Nothing ...
Jacqui Can't bear what, though, my love?
Liz Well ... everything ...
Jacqui You look most peculiar.
Liz No, it's just that ...

Hilary comes back from the corridor, putting on her overcoat

Jacqui What?
Liz Forget it, forget it.

Liz goes back into the library

Jacqui (*to Hilary*) Off, then, are you, my sweet?
Hilary Unless there's anything else ... ?
Jacqui No, no. Off you go. It's been absolutely lovely having you here, my precious.
Hilary Lovely being here. (*Calling*) Good-night, Terry! Good-night, Liz!

Terry appears from his office

Terry Night, night, then, Hil. Get your breath back. Big week coming up.

Liz appears in the doorway of the library

Hilary Yes. Good-night, Jacqui.
Jacqui Have an absolutely super weekend.
Hilary I will.
Terry Don't do anything I wouldn't.

Hilary goes out of the main door

Jacqui turns decisively to Terry

Jacqui Terry, listen ...

Terry looks at Liz. Jacqui looks as well

Liz disappears back into the library

Jacqui shuts the library door

Hilary ...
Terry What about her?
Jacqui You know what she's doing every time she gets half a chance?

Pause

Terry No? What's she doing?
Jacqui She's writing some sort of report about the way the Home Office
    works. I had a look when she was out of the room today. Terry, my love,
    she's putting in everyone's names — all the people she used to work with.
    She's saying what part they all played in the Hassam thing. Did you know
    about this?
Terry No. No, I didn't.
Jacqui Well, you're going to have to be very firm with her, my darling.
    Because, Terry, if we did anything that got her into trouble ...
Terry Listen, I feel just the same as you ...
Jacqui The Home Office security people are going to interview her again
    tomorrow. They know something's up ... You're *not* going to do anything
    silly with that file, are you?
Terry Aren't I?
Jacqui Terry, you *couldn't*! You *couldn't*! Not now we know her! Not now
    she's one of us!
Terry No ...
Jacqui Terry!

Terry Yes, but she wants us to. She wants us to use it.
Jacqui But you know what'll happen! You said yourself!
Terry She don't care. She wants us to.
Jacqui You've talked to her about it?
Terry Long talk.
Jacqui When was this? I haven't seen you talking to her.
Terry Last night.
Jacqui I was here last night.
Terry After you'd gone. She come back to the office. Left her bag behind.

Pause

What's that supposed to mean?
Jacqui What?
Terry That look?
Jacqui Terry ... you have still got it?
Terry Got it? What, the file?
Jacqui Where is it?
Terry You don't trust me?
Jacqui I just want to see it.

He goes into his office

(*Softly*) I know you, my sweetheart.

He comes back holding up the file

Terry I gave it to her, my old love! You fetched it back!
Jacqui Terry, she's in a very strange state!
Terry Funny old state *you're* in, my love, never mind her.
Jacqui Yes, but something's happened, I don't know what it is. I think she's probably had some truly ghastly bust-up with Roy. You know she hasn't even told him she was working here? You haven't said anything to her about ... ?
Terry What?
Jacqui Us.
Terry No? Why?
Jacqui Something she said. I know it's silly, but I just feel we ought to be a bit ... careful. Well, I remember the way Poops reacted when you first came out to Sunningdale. I don't think children want to know too much about what their parents get up to.
Terry We're not her parents! Keep saying it to yourself! We're not her parents!

Jacqui Yes, but I expect she's a bit soft on you herself, you see, my darling. She's terribly careful never to look at you. Haven't you noticed?

She goes out to the corridor

(*Off*) Well, even Poops has a funny thing about her father, I'm perfectly well aware of that, though she'd die rather than admit it to me.

She comes back with her overcoat, and moves towards the main door

Anyway, all the girls still go a bit woozy when they see you, as you well know, and of course they do, because you're a very attractive man, and you're more than that, you're a great man, and I told her so, and don't you take advantage of it ... (*She looks at the file*) We shouldn't keep that in the office. What happens if we get Special Branch round with a search warrant again?

Terry Still secret?

Jacqui Well, it is.

Terry Yes ...

Jacqui We're not leaving it here over the weekend?

Terry (*thinking*) No ... (*He offers it to her*) Take it home with you.

Jacqui Me?

Terry Hide it away somewhere. Safe from them. Safe from me.

Jacqui Aren't you coming?

Terry Coming where?

Jacqui Home!

Terry (*remembering*) Oh, what, Poops — she's back for the hols?

Jacqui You hadn't forgotten?

Terry Course I hadn't forgotten. (*He doesn't move*)

Jacqui What?

Terry Nothing. (*He pats his pocket*) Wallet. Go on down. I'll catch you up.

Jacqui She'd be so disappointed.

Terry I'm coming!

She goes out

He thinks, then pushes open the library door, still holding the file

Liz ...

Liz comes anxiously out of the library

Terry You here for a bit?

Liz It's Friday.
Terry Tidying everything up for us?
Liz Just the usual.
Terry Right, so anyone wants to know where I am ...
Liz You'll be away tonight.
Terry Old Poops. It's her half-term.
Liz I know.
Terry Can't be helped.
Liz No.
Terry (*thinking*) Just tell them ... No, put it like this ... No, say I'll phone them.
Liz Phone them, right.
Terry You'll lock up, then?
Liz Yes.

He opens the main door, and stands there for a moment, looking at the file he is holding

Terry All getting a bit deep for me, this, Liz.
Liz (*laughing bleakly*) All getting a bit deep for all of us.
Terry Yes. Sorry about that.

She looks at the file

Liz It looks like a bomb, the way you're holding it.
Terry What, this?
Liz What are you going to do with it?
Terry I don't know, Liz. I don't know.
Liz Throw it.
Terry Blow up a lot of things if I did.
Liz Why not? Blow up everything.
Terry People we know.
Liz If we're serious about Mr Hassam.
Terry Mr Hassam's dead. Other people aren't.
Liz Also we didn't know him.
Terry Makes a difference, Liz.
Liz Does it?
Terry Doesn't it?

Pause

Liz So you're taking it away?
Terry Put it somewhere safe.
Liz In Jacqui's house? (*She laughs*)

Terry (*ruefully*) Right.

She holds out her hand for the file

Give it to you?
Liz Neutral territory.
Terry (*thinking*) No, I'll put it back where it was.

He takes the file back into his office and returns

Dangerous things, bombs. Less they get moved around the better. (*He closes his office door*) So you'll tell them, if they come?
Liz Tell who?
Terry Them.
Liz Oh, them.
Terry OK. You're a pal. (*He goes to the main door*)
Liz And tomorrow night?
Terry We'll see how it goes.
Liz And Sunday night?
Terry We'll see, tell them. We'll see.

Terry goes

Liz sits down in Jacqui's chair, turns on the computer, and opens all the files that Jacqui has just closed. Then she goes back to the main door, opens it, and listens. The sound of the street door closing three flights below. She closes the door and goes into Terry's office

The main door opens, and Hilary looks in cautiously. She crosses to Terry's office and listens, then smiles to herself

Hilary Wait! Don't come out till I tell you! (*She turns away and quickly starts to undress, without taking off her overcoat*)

Liz emerges from Terry's office, holding Hilary's file

I said wait ... ! (*She looks back and see that it is Liz. She pulls the overcoat around herself*)

Pause

Liz He's not here. He's had to go away for the night.
Hilary No, I just came back to ...

Pause

Liz Catch up on some work. Right.
Hilary I'm sorry.
Liz No, no.

Hilary notices the file in Liz's hands

I was fetching your file. Terry told me to look after it.

She goes to Jacqui's seat, and begins to work on Jacqui's files. Hilary goes uncertainly to her own part of the desk

Hilary And Terry's had to ... ?
Liz Go away somewhere. He said he'd phone. If anyone asked for him.

Pause

Hilary Thank you, anyway.

Pause

It's very nice of you. I realize it's all rather ... awkward.
Liz Not at all.
Hilary Well, it is.
Liz Yes, but so's everything.
Hilary Is it?
Liz Don't you find?

Pause

Hilary Not always.
Liz No?
Hilary Not usually.
Liz When you come back to catch up on your work?
Hilary Yes.
Liz Good. I'm glad. (*She works*)
Hilary What are you doing?
Liz (*grinning*) Oh ... tidying up.
Hilary But isn't that ...
Liz What — Jacqui's? Yes!

Pause

You mean, should we be messing around with Jacqui's things?

Hilary No, I was simply wondering ...

Liz works on, grinning

Liz It's the newsletter. She won't use the spell-checker. I don't know why not. And she hates anyone else looking at what she's done — I always have to go through everything when she's not here. It's so silly — she knows perfectly well I do it. People are funny, aren't they? It can't go out like this, though. Do you want to see?

Hilary shakes her head. Pause

Hilary Just tonight?
Liz He didn't know. He said he'd see how it went. (*She laughs*) This is her appeal for funds. Listen: "Come on all you affulent types ... "

Liz laughs. Hilary does not

"*Affulent* ... " I can just see them, can't you? All our affulent supporters. At one of those lunch meetings that Terry has to go and talk to, probably. Somehow affable and flatulent at the same time, sort of burping benevolence.

Liz laughs Hilary does not

Sorry. Sorry ... There are some things you can't tell people, though, aren't there. Some things you have to let them find out for themselves. Don't you think?

Pause

Hilary Gone where?
Liz I don't know. Oh no, this is a classic! "Let's make next month's appeal figures a real *banasa* ... "
Hilary Bonanza?
Liz I suppose. I had a wild picture of some sort of specially squashy banana.
Hilary You mean she's dyslexic?
Liz Or *disexic*. That's what she said in one of her editorials. "Hold on to your seats chaps the poor old Ed's a raging disexic." Sorry! I keep all these things to myself usually.
Hilary Disexic ... (*She smiles slightly, and relaxes enough to button up her shirt*)
Liz Quite funny, though, having someone who's disexic to edit the newsletter. Don't you think? It's the same with the accounts. She won't use

the spreadsheet, I don't know why not. It makes Terry so cross! She does them all by hand, on odd bits of paper. Then she takes them off to a *little man* down in Sunningdale. She's got all kinds of *little men* working away for her down there. It's like *Snow White and the Seven Dwarfs*. Anyway, her little man lays them out and makes them look all right — I don't know how — she never lets anyone else see them — certainly not me — I don't think even Terry — she keeps them under lock and key ... (*She pulls at the drawer in the desk in front of her to demonstrate*) You see? Quite funny, having someone who can't do accounts to do the accounts. Don't you think?

Hilary I get the impression she lives with someone.

Liz laughs

Or perhaps not all the time. She's very mysterious about it. She never refers to him directly. I thought possibly he was ...

Pause. Liz waits

I don't know. Someone else's husband. Or the gardener, or something.

Liz resumes work

No?

Liz gets up. She fetches the wire coat-hanger that Terry's shirt was on. She holds it up for Hilary to see, smiling

Hilary (*puzzled*) Coat-hanger?

Liz Haven't you ever picked a lock? (*She laughs, and picks the lock of Jacqui's drawer*)

Hilary Listen, I don't think we should ...

Liz Yes, we should, if she keeps it locked. Don't you want to find out about all our little mysteries?

Hilary Liz, don't ... don't.

Liz I've done it! (*She takes the drawer out and puts it on the desk*) Aren't we awful?

Hilary (*seriously*) Yes, we are.

But she watches, fascinated, as Liz goes through the contents

Liz I hate looking in someone else's things! Don't you? I just want to run out of the room ... (*She searches avidly among the contents, and pulls out a* *small child's painting)* "My Mummy"! Aren't we horrible? (*She takes out some picture postcards*) More Poops. "I'm having a brill time. The food is yucky. Inez was sick in Fiona's ski boot. We all hate the French."

Hilary puts her envelope down, and looks in the drawer. She takes out an exercise book

Two odd gloves ... Four old pennies ... Receipts ... VAT invoices ...
Hilary These are the accounts.

Liz takes out a spiral-bound shorthand book and looks inside it

Liz I think this is the payroll ...
Hilary Subscriptions ... covenants ... There doesn't seem to be very much money coming in ...
Liz Do you want to know what we all earn?
Hilary No, thank you.
Liz It's funny what people don't want to know about.
Hilary I don't see how we keep going on this income ... I suppose she was ... having some kind of affair with him. Was she? Is that how it all started?
Liz (*laughing*) I'll make us some coffee. (*She goes to the kettle and switches it on*)
Hilary And now he feels he can't just push her out ...
Liz Anyway, never mind.
Hilary Nothing to do with me.
Liz Listen, why don't we leave all this nonsense? (*She turns off the kettle*) You look a bit tired. We'll go out and see a film. (*She quickly puts everything back in the drawer*)
Hilary Why never mind?
Liz Nothing. You could come back to my place afterwards — we could have something to eat.
Hilary Well, that's very kind, only I've got to do various things ...
Liz Come on! Jacqui told me to borrow you! (*She fits the drawer back into the desk*) It's funny, really. She keeps all this mess inside her desk ... (*She slams the drawer home*) ... but you should have seen her when she found those broken biscuits!

Hilary looks away

Sorry! (*She clamps her hand over her mouth*) Lock it up again.

Hilary watches her sombrely as she tries to relock the drawer with the coat-hanger

It opened like a dream — I don't know why it won't ... Doesn't matter — she'll think she left it like this herself ... (*She hides the remains of the coathanger in the waste-paper basket under some newspapers*) On second thoughts ...

Liz takes it out again, and goes out with it into the corridor. She reappears inside the mailroom, holds up a waste-paper basket, grinning, and puts the coat-hanger into it. She returns putting on her overcoat

Kevin's! She won't look there ... Terrible pair we are!

She switches off the computer, and puts Hilary's coat around her shoulders for her

You went such a lovely red, though! When Shireen said.
Hilary Said what?
Liz About the biscuits.

She propels Hilary towards the main door

Anyway, never mind. Don't worry about it! But I think you'll find he's usually got things to do at the weekend.
Hilary You mean ... ?
Liz Anyway, there's always Chrissie's room. The girl I share with. She's away a lot at the weekend ... Oh, the file! (*She runs back and fetches it*) We'll take it with us. We can look after it together.

They go out

CURTAIN

SCENE 2

The same. Day

Shireen is on the switch. Kent and Kevin are in the mailroom. Hilary is working at her desk. The door to the library is open

Jacqui enters through the main door

Jacqui That doorway ... ! (*To Hilary*) Hallo, my precious.
Hilary (*coolly*) Hallo.
Jacqui Lovely weekend?

Hilary Thank you. And you?
Jacqui Funny smell in here ... Oh, you know, family life ... What *is* that smell ...? No, we all had a lovely time.

Shireen slides back her screen

Shireen Oh, Jacqui, that Steven person rang for Terry again ...
Jacqui Yes, yes — only don't go away, Shireen. Something I want to say to you.

Liz appears in the doorway of the library

Jacqui puts her handbag down on her desk

(*To Hilary*) Are you all right, my love?
Hilary Fine.
Jacqui Only you look a bit funny somehow. Doesn't she, Liz?

Liz laughs

A little *beaky*. Nothing's happened?
Hilary No.
Jacqui Not something over the weekend ... ?
Hilary No.
Jacqui No, well, it's probably just the weather. Or the smell ...
Liz What smell?
Jacqui Can't you smell it?
Shireen What's it like, Jacqui?
Jacqui Different. Now, Shireen! (*She takes off her overcoat*) I come in on a freezing Monday morning to start what's obviously going to be a horrendous week, what with the Hassam thing, and our great lobby coming up tomorrow, and what do I find?

She takes her overcoat out through the corridor door

Shireen (*to Liz and Hilary*) Oh, no! I forgot the doorway again!
Liz (*to Shireen*) I'll do it! (*She goes to the main door*)

Jacqui comes back without the overcoat

Jacqui I find that doorway downstairs in the most incredible state.
Liz I'm going, I'm going!
Jacqui I mean *clean*.

Liz (*stopping*) Clean?
Jacqui No cardboard, no cans, no congealed food on paper plates — nothing.
So thank you, Shireen!
Shireen Oh, well ... I do *try* to remember, Jacqui.
Jacqui Good. Well done! We've got the week off to a lovely start for once.
And Kent's not picking his nose. Kevin's not scratching himself ... (*She
stops, looking at something under her desk*)
Shireen What — the smell?
Liz What sort of smell is it?
Shireen Nice? Nasty?

Jacqui bends down and picks up two used cardboard plates under her desk

Liz What?
Shireen What is it, Jacqui?
Jacqui Spaghetti. Apparently. In tomato sauce.
Liz Oh, no.
Shireen Oh, Jacqui, how awful!
Jacqui Shireen, my love, I didn't mean to take the rubbish out of the doorway
and put it under my desk!
Shireen I didn't!
Jacqui That's an absolutely cretinous thing to do!
Shireen It wasn't me, Jacqui, honestly!
Jacqui I've got this muck all over my hands now!

*She drops the plate in the waste-paper basket and rushes out of the door
to the corridor*

Shireen I didn't put anything under her desk!
Liz Don't worry.
Shireen But whatever I do it's wrong! I say I didn't do the doorway — she
goes mad! I say I did do it — she goes madder still!
Liz What does it matter?
Shireen It's so unfair!

The phone buzzes

"Thank you, Shireen" — then two minutes later it's as bad as last week ...
(*Into the headset*) Hallo, OPEN ...
Liz (*to Hilary*) *You* did it?
Hilary Me? The doorway? No.
Liz Another mystery. (*She looks in Jacqui's handbag*)
Hilary What — her keys?

Liz Get the drawer locked up! That'll be the next thing!

Jacqui comes back in, even angrier than when she went out

Jacqui Where is it?

Liz moves away from the handbag

Liz What?

But Jacqui is looking at the door, not the handbag

Jacqui The coat-hanger!
Liz The coat-hanger?

Liz and Hilary look at each other. Jacqui bangs on Shireen's screen. Shireen opens it

Jacqui Shireen, my sweet ...
Shireen (*into the headset*) Hold on ...
Jacqui There was a wire coat-hanger hanging here on Friday. Where is it?
Shireen Oh, Jacqui, I don't know, I haven't seen it ... A wire coat-hanger?
Jacqui Yes! I need it, you see.
Shireen You need a coat-hanger?
Jacqui To unblock the lavatory.
Shireen Oh, no!
Jacqui I won't describe the state the room's in.
Shireen Oh, poor Jacqui, what a morning! Have you asked the boys?

Jacqui turns to look at the mailroom. Kent and Kevin who have stopped to watch events in the main office, quickly resume whatever they were doing

Jacqui Only of course it won't be them. It's never them. It's never anyone.
Hilary (*to Jacqui*) I don't think it's Kevin or Kent ...
Jacqui (*to Hilary*) Don't worry, my precious — I'm not going to eat them! But *no-one* in this office will ever admit *responsibility* for anything. It absolutely *enrages* me.

She goes out of the corridor door again, and appears in the mailroom

Shireen It's Kevin, isn't it ... (*She emerges from the switch to watch*) He's always doing funny things with things. Oh, she's really, really going for him! You can't watch, can you, only you kind of can't stop ...

Hilary (*to Liz*) We'll have to tell her.
Liz Wait! Wait!

She searches through Jacqui's bag. Shireen gazes at the mailroom

Shireen It's in his bag, it's in his bag ... He won't show her! He's hanging
on for dear life! (*She sees what Liz is doing*) What?
Liz (*laughing*) Nothing.
Shireen That's Jacqui's.
Liz I was just looking for something.
Shireen What's going on? I don't know what's going on here this morning!

Liz takes her hands away from Jacqui's bag, shamed by Shireen's scrutiny

I don't know what Hilary's going to think.
Hilary (*looking at the mailroom*) She's found it.
Shireen Oh, no!

*Jacqui is gesturing with the remains of the wire coat-hanger that she has
extracted from Kevin's waste-paper bin*

In his bag?
Hilary In his waste-paper basket.

Jacqui disappears from the mailroom

Liz, we'll have to say ...
Shireen (*to Hilary*) Yes, because you've never seen Jacqui like this before,
have you? Oh, poor Hilary! (*To Liz*) She thinks we're all mad! (*To Hilary*)
She'll have a go at you next! Won't she, Liz?
Liz Probably. If we don't get everything else right ...

*She puts her hand into Jacqui's handbag again while Shireen is talking to
Hilary*

Shireen You were so thick together last week, but that won't stop her! So were
Jacqui and Liz once! Weren't you, Liz? She falls out with everyone, that
woman, it's a shame, because if it's not like friendly here, I mean, what's the
point? You'd rather leave, wouldn't you, you'd rather do audio ...

Jacqui enters from the corridor

Jacqui Shireen ...

Liz moves away from the handbag

Hilary (*to Jacqui*) That coat-hanger.
Jacqui (*to Hilary*) One moment, my love ... Shireen, is it you who blocked the lavatory?
Shireen Blocked the lavatory? Not me, Jacqui, I haven't been in there.
Jacqui (*to Liz*) There's no need to go snittering and jittering! I don't want to hold a court of inquiry, I don't want to blame anyone. I simply want to find out what happened so we can stop it happening again.
Shireen It was probably just Kevin, you know what he's like.
Jacqui Yes, but whatever Kevin gets up to in there, I don't think he'd put a sanitary towel down the loo. Let alone two sanitary towels together.
Shireen Oh, Jacqui, no! (*She puts her hands over her face, embarrassed*)
Jacqui Oh, Jacqui, *yes*! Now, Shireen ...
Hilary I think this is probably my fault.
Jacqui (*to Hilary, irritated*) Oh, don't *you* start, my darling! It's maddening enough when Liz does it! I'm not going to be angry with her. I just want to *know*. (*To Shireen*) Now listen, my precious ...
Hilary Tina and Donna.
Jacqui What?
Hilary The two in the doorway. I said they could sleep in here last night.
Shireen Oh, no!
Liz (*laughing in surprise*) Sorry ... The smell ... Sorry ... (*She hides her face in her hands*)
Shireen And the plates ...
Hilary I should have mentioned it before ...
Jacqui I don't understand.
Hilary Those two girls.
Shireen They slept in here!
Liz On the floor?
Hilary There was a frost last night.
Jacqui (*to Hilary*) What are you saying, my love? You're not saying that you ... *invited* them in?
Liz (*laughing*) Sorry ....
Jacqui (*to Liz*) You knew about this, did you?
Liz (*laughing*) No!
Jacqui (*to Hilary*) So you took it upon yourself ... ?
Hilary I told them to be out this morning before anyone arrived.
Jacqui (*smiling with anger*) My honey ... My dear sweet girl ...
Hilary I'm sorry. I should have made sure they'd left the place tidy.
Jacqui I know you've been working in this office for all of a *week*, my darling ...
Hilary There was no-one here to consult, so I had to make a decision ...

Jacqui Yes, but I don't imagine you'd have invited people in off the street in your *last* place of employment!

Hilary But if you've got an organization that believes in openness ...

Terry comes in through the main door, holding a number of clean shirts on hangers

Jacqui (*to Hilary*) No, my darling! No! No! No!

Hilary ... we can't really keep our doors locked ...

Jacqui No! Listen to what I'm telling you! *No!*

Hilary ... when there are people outside who may die ...

Jacqui *No!* Quite simply — *no!*

Shireen (*to Terry*) Those girls! They spent the night in here!

The phone begins to buzz

Hilary (*to Jacqui*) Listen ...

Jacqui (*eyes closed*) No! I'm sorry! No! No! No!

Terry (*calmly*) OK, end of argument ...

Jacqui (*to Hilary*) No! You see? No! No!

Terry I said end of argument. Shireen, you get back on the switch, the phone's going. Liz, this don't concern you.

Shireen returns to the switch

Shireen (*into the headset*) Hallo, OPEN ... (*She closes the window*)

Liz goes back into the library

Terry Right, back to work. All over and done with. No need to go on about it because it's not going to happen again. (*Unhurriedly, he hangs up his shirts*)

Jacqui (*to Hilary*) Last night? What do you mean, you let them in *last night*? Last night was Sunday!

Terry Never mind about that ...

Jacqui No, but what was she doing here?

Hilary I came in. I had some work to do.

Jacqui Work? What work? (*She turns over the papers on Hilary's desk*)

Hilary (*closing the file*) Just some work of my own.

Jacqui (*opening it*) This is your file. These are the things you sent to Terry.

Hilary I'm annotating it. I thought we could hand out copies at our lobby tomorrow.

Jacqui But Terry said he left it in his office.

Shireen slides back her window

Shireen Terry ...
Jacqui (*to Terry*) You said you put this back in your office.
Terry (*to Jacqui*) Hold on, hold on ...
Shireen (*to Terry*) It's Peter someone.
Terry (*to Shireen*) Not now, love.

Shireen waits, interested

(*To Jacqui*) Let's take this nice and gentle.
Hilary Liz gave it to me.
Jacqui Liz gave it to you? But this is ridiculous? (*Calling*) Liz! (*To Hilary*)
When did she give this to you?

Liz emerges from the library

Hilary Over the weekend.
Jacqui Over the weekend? Last night? You were both here?
Hilary On Friday night.

Jacqui looks from one to the other

Jacqui I don't understand. What's going on?
Hilary I think we ought to publish this material.
Jacqui And you were going to do it behind all our backs?
Hilary No, I thought we should all talk about it and decide together.
Jacqui Oh, *did* you, my darling?
Terry Fair enough. We got to get it thrashed out sooner or later. Why not
now? It's going to take all morning, though, so let's get ourselves sat down
before we start.

Hilary sits down at her desk

Liz ...

Liz sits

(*To Jacqui*) And you, my love.

Jacqui reluctantly sits

Shireen Terry ...

Terry (*to Shireen*) I said, not now. Tell him.

Shireen reluctantly closes her window

Right. (*He sits down himself*) Let's have a proper debate. Are we going to publish Hilary's file or aren't we? I call on Hilary to speak first, tell us what *she* thinks. Go on, then, Hilary.

Jacqui (*to Hilary*) Who gave you the keys?

Hilary The keys?

Jacqui To this office.

Hilary No-one.

Jacqui No-one? What do you mean, "no-one"?

Hilary I had a set.

Terry *I* gave them to her. Last week. Right — Hilary.

Hilary (*to Jacqui*) I don't know what you're worrying about. I wasn't here with *him*.

Jacqui With Terry?

Hilary You know I wasn't. At least, *assume* you know I wasn't. Since he was with you. Wasn't he?

Jacqui What do you mean? Why should he be here?

Hilary Why should he be here? Because this is where he usually is at night.

Jacqui (*puzzled*) Yes ... ?

Terry Never mind all that. Just tell us about this file of yours, Hilary. How can we publish it without dropping you in it ... ?

Hilary (*to Jacqui*) I'm just saying — Friday night, Saturday night, last night — he *wasn't*.

Pause

Jacqui (*quietly*) I'm going out for a walk. I don't feel very well.

She goes out through the main door

Hilary (*to Terry*) I'm sorry. But you *weren't*!

Terry (*quietly, not looking at Hilary*) I'd better take her her coat. She'll catch her death out there this morning.

He goes out to the corridor

Liz (*to Hilary*) Well done!

Hilary I didn't mean it like that!

Liz Are you all right?

Terry reappears from the corridor, carrying Jacqui's coat. Liz melts back into the library

Hilary (*to Terry*) Anyway, she'd have had to face up to it sooner or later.
Terry Right ... Though I don't know why sooner or later always has to mean sooner.

Terry goes out of the main door

Hilary Wait ...

Hilary runs out after him. Liz comes out of the library

Shireen opens her screen

Shireen (*to Liz*) My know-all sister! "But Shireen," she goes, "nothing ever happens in that office!"

The phone buzzes

(*Into the headset*) Hallo, OPEN ...

Liz opens the main door, then stops

Terry (*off*) ... Hil, I been ringing your number all weekend! I rang you seven times ...!

Liz shuts the door again

Shireen (*into the headset*) No, he's out ...

Liz discreetly returns to her search of Jacqui's handbag

No, she's out — they're all out — there's only Liz ... (*She turns to Liz; calling*) Liz!

Liz quickly takes her hands out of Jacqui's bag

(*To Liz*) Oh, sorry ...

Liz goes back to the main door, and looks cautiously out

(*To Liz*) Only it's that man in television about the lobby tomorrow ...

Liz grins and shakes her head, and goes out

(*Into the headset*) No, sorry — *she's* going out as well — they've all gone mad this morning ... !

Kent runs in from the corridor door towards the switch, holding Kevin's haversack

Kent Hey, Shireen! Kevin's got this picture of you in his bag with no clothes on!

Kevin comes in from the corridor door

Kevin No! No!

He chases Kent ineffectually around the desk

Kent What? That one where they're doing it on the motor-bike! You said it looked like Shireen!
Kevin (*desperately*) I didn't ... !

Shireen emerges from the switch

Shireen Now don't you two start!
Kent It's Kev! He's got all these wicked books!

He pulls magazines out of the haversack to show Shireen. Kevin struggles to stop him

Kevin Give me ... Give me ...
Kent Look at him! He's a crazy man!
Shireen Yes, well, don't tease him.
Kent I'm not. I'm cheering him up! Well pissed off, he was!
Kevin Give me that ...
Kent Did something weird with her coat-hanger, didn't you, Kev? Old Jacqui was giving him all kinds of grief.
Shireen Look, will you two stop messing around!
Kent Hey, look at this one, Shireen ...
Kevin Give me that ... Give me that ...

He lunges at Kent, who jumps on to the desk to keep the magazines out of Kevin's reach. He tramples back and forth over the files and papers, while Kevin flaps ineffectually around his knees

Kent No, she'll love it, Kev! She'll know you fancy her!

Kevin I don't ... I don't ...

Kent You *don't* fancy her? Shireen, Kev don't fancy you no more! What, it's Hilary now, is it, you wicked man?

Shireen Get out of here, the pair of you! I've had nothing but messing around ever since I came in this morning!

The phone buzzes

I'm sick of it! Now my phone's going ...

She starts back to the switch, but is distracted by Kevin's dislodging Jacqui's handbag

And that's her bag!

Kevin grabs at the bag to save it, and the contents empty over the edge of the desk on to the floor

Kent Oh, now you done it, Kevvy!

Kevin and Shireen try to recover the contents of the handbag. Kent tips the contents of the haversack over their heads. The phone goes on buzzing

Here you are, you bad boy! Bums and bazoombas everywhere! Hey, no, get this one! (*He throws the haversack away and recovers one of the magazines from the desk*)

Liz and Hilary enter through the main door and stop short at the sight

I think this one's Hilary! Look! Look! Down over the desk, darling ... !

He becomes aware of Liz and Hilary, and is instantly inert. Kevin and Shireen straighten up as well. The phone stops buzzing. Silence

Hilary (*quietly*) Get off there, will you please, Kent. That's my desk. Those are my papers.

Kent gets down

Shireen Just half a chance, that's all they need, these two!

Liz picks up some of the things that Shireen and Kent have recovered

Liz Is this all out of Jacqui's bag?
Shireen They're always coming in here making trouble!

Liz gets down on the floor, pushing the magazines aside. She hands Hilary some papers

Liz This is out of your file ... But where are her keys? There should be some keys.
Shireen I told them! I begged them!

Kevin, still kneeling, is holding the magazines he has recovered. He looks round for the haversack. Hilary takes the magazines out his hands

Hilary Thank you, Kevin.
Kevin Oh ... Oh ...
Hilary (*to Kent*) These are yours, are they?

Kent shrugs. Kevin looks at Hilary's feet

Kevin I won't ... I don't ... I won't ... I don't ...
Hilary Just a moment, Kevin. I'm talking to Kent.

Kevin looks up, mouth open

(*To Kent*) I said, these are your magazines, are they, Kent?
Kent (*blankly*) No.
Hilary So what are you doing with them?
Kent Found them.
Hilary You found them. Oh. Found them where?
Kent Lying around.
Hilary Where — in the office?
Kent Don't know.
Shireen He goes, "Look at these, Shireen!"
Hilary So whose are they, Kent? Not Shireen's?

Kent shrugs

Mine? Liz's? Kevin's?

Kent shrugs

Kevin I think ...

Hilary Now, Kent, I know Terry's out. I know I've only been working here for a week. But there are some strange things going on in this office, and I've a pretty shrewd idea what's happening in that mailroom for a start. So let's all agree — no more harassment and no more bullying. Yes? Take this stuff away, then, Kent, and look at it in private, if that's the best you can manage, but don't ever bring anything like it into the office again. (*She throws the magazines down on the desk in front of Kent, and wipes her hands with a tissue*) Now we've all got a lot of work to do ...
Kevin In all fairness ...
Hilary (*slightly impatient*) What is it, Kevin?
Kevin In all fairness ...

The main door begins to open

Jacqui (*off*) I don't want to know! All right? I simply *don't want to know*! I don't want to think about it ... !

Jacqui comes in, followed by Terry. She goes straight to the corridor to hang up her coat without looking at the others

Terry *Now* what's happening? The Christmas party?
Kevin No ...
Terry No. Right. So let's get some work done this morning.
Kevin I was just ...
Terry Back in the mailroom, Kevin.

Kevin obeys

And you, Kent.

Kent turns to go

Hilary (*to Kent*) Yes, and take these with you.

She picks up the magazines and gives them to him

Terry Hold on. What's all this?
Liz Nothing.
Hilary It's all over.
Terry What are them mags?
Hilary Nothing!

Jacqui comes back in from the corridor

Terry (*to Jacqui*) Nothing. That's what they're all doing.

Jacqui shrugs, turn on the kettle, and fills a mug of hot water to wrap her hands around. Kent moves towards the corridor door with the magazines

Nothing. Well, that sounds all right.

Shireen sobs

Hold on a moment, though, Kent.

Kent stops

Shireen don't look too happy about it all.
Shireen I don't want to work here any more.
Terry You what?
Shireen I don't want to work in this kind of office! I don't want to get all upset! I just want to know what I'm supposed to do, and get on and do it. You say like, "We're talking about secret things, you mustn't listen." So all right — I don't listen. You say like, "We're all going to be in trouble." All right — so we're all going to be in trouble? I don't mind! You tell me — I'll do it! I just don't want people like being horrible all the time!

She goes out to the corridor

Terry Now, listen, Shireen, my darling. I don't know what's been going on in here ...

She comes back holding her overcoat

Shireen I know people don't always agree. I know they've got sad things in their life. *I* don't always agree. *I've* got sad things in *my* life. But I don't go round like telling everyone and spoiling things for them ...

Terry puts his arm around her

Terry Come on, Shireen ...

She pushes Terry away

Shireen If people can't get on I don't think they ought to like argue and make trouble for everyone. I think they just ought to like put on their coat and go. (*She puts her coat on*)

Terry sits down in Jacqui's chair and calmly raises his hand

Terry Not so fast, Shireen. I want to get to the bottom of this. Let's hear from Kent. He's the expert on nothing. What sort of nothing's been going on here, Kent?

Kent shrugs

Kent Don't want to work in that room no more.
Terry Oh. You don't want to work in that room no more. So why's that, then, Kent?
Kent Don't want to work with *him* no more.
Terry You don't want to work with Kevin? Why don't you want to work with Kevin?
Kent Just don't.
Terry Just don't. All right, Kent. So what you want me to say? Can't take Kevin out of there, can I, because what else can he do? Can't take *you* out, because what else can you do?

Kent shrugs. The phone begins to buzz

Kent Go on the switch.
Terry Go on the switch? You want to go on the switch?

Kent shrugs

Funny, isn't it. First time I ever asked you something and you knew the answer. Well, that's a crying shame, my friend, cause the answer's wrong. No, you can't go on the switch. OK?
Kent Buzzing.
Terry Yes, and it's going to go on buzzing, I'm afraid, Kent.
Jacqui (*sharply*) Where's my bag?
Kent So why can't I go on it?
Terry Hold on, Kent. Jacqui's bag ... (*He picks it up from the floor where Kevin and Shireen left it, and hands it to Jacqui*) Right, that's one problem solved. (*To Kent*) Now, why can't you go on the switch ...? (*He bends down again automatically to pick up something else he has noticed on the floor. It's one of Kevin's magazines. He looks at it*)

The phone stops buzzing

Oh, I see. That's what it's all about. (*He throws the magazine down on the desk*) Now, listen, Kent. I don't like this kind of muck. If I was in the Home

Office I'd have it all seized and burnt. Funny, coming from me? OK, laugh away, but there's a limit to everything. Everything? Everything. So, Kent, old son, drop all that garbage in the bin.

He waits while Kent puts the magazines he is holding into the black plastic bag lining the waste-paper bin

Right. Now. Listen, Kent ...

Jacqui Someone's been going through my bag! All the things are mixed up and broken!

Hilary Your bag got knocked off the table. We had to put everything back as best we could.

Jacqui I can't bear people touching my things! (*To Terry*) Get away from my desk! Get away! Go on! Out!

Terry gets up

They haven't been into my drawer ... ?

She shoves Terry aside, and yanks at her drawer. It opens without resistance — comes right out in her hand and scatters the contents everywhere

Oh *no*! It was *locked*! I left it *locked*!! I keep it *locked*! Which if you did this? Which of you broke into my drawer? (*To Kent*) This was you, was it? Or was it Kevin? Was this with the coat-hanger? It was both of you!

Hilary It was me. I did it on Friday evening. I wanted to see what you'd got in there. It was very stupid and very wrong of me. I shouldn't have done it. I'm sorry.

Jacqui You?

Liz Well, me, actually. (*She laughs*) And I put the coat-hanger in Kevin's waste-paper basket afterwards.

Hilary We did it together.

Jacqui Together? Together? What have I ever done to you? What have I ever done to either of you?

Terry (*calmly*) Now, let's take this very slow and very calm. Let's all see if we can somehow get this rusty old aeroplane back on the ground again ...

The main door opens, and Roy enters

They all turn to look at him. He stops short at the sight of them all assembled

Roy Oh ... More participatory democracy?

Terry Right.

Roy Admirable. (*He advances into the room and places a typescript on the desk*) Secrecy in the legal profession. My report. I promised I'd bring it in.

Terry (*preoccupied*) OK, Roy. Thanks.

Roy So ... everyone except Kevin. And me.

Terry Sit down. Join in the fun.

Roy (*declining*) I'll leave you with a written contribution instead. (*He takes an envelope out of his pocket, and places it on top of the report*)

Terry (*picking it up*) What this, Roy?

Roy A personal note.

Terry opens it and reads it

Well, I imagine you can dispense with *my* services now, can't you?

Terry Oh, I see ... No, we'd be very sorry to lose you, Roy, you know that.

Roy But since you've appointed a full-time professional consultant of your own ... (*Formally*) Hallo, Hilary.

Hilary (*formally*) Hallo.

Roy And since you even did *that* without needing any advice from me ... Without even asking me for a reference, which is a little curious, since I knew the applicant personally. Without so much as telling me you'd done it. I only found out over the weekend. (*To Hilary*) From one of your former colleagues. Ironically enough.

Terry Roy, can we talk about this some other time?

Roy Of course. (*He picks up the file from Hilary's desk and begins to look through it*)

The phone begins to buzz. No-one moves. Roy looks up, first at the switch, then at Shireen, who has not moved

Oh, I see. Things are obviously changing around here. Your new consultant is plainly taking the organization in hand.

Terry We're busy, Roy.

Roy Internal matters?

Terry Off you go, then, old lad.

Roy (*looking through the file*) This is what you're all talking about, is it?

Terry closes the file up and takes it out of Roy's hands

Oh — secret?

Terry I'll be in touch.

Roy laughs, and goes to the door

Roy She's certainly making her mark. I could have told you. If you'd asked me.

Terry Right. Cheers.

The phone stops buzzing

Roy Perhaps OPEN'S not quite the right name any more. How about SHUT?

Roy goes out

Terry keeps the file in his hands

Shireen You see? It used to be nice here, it used to be friendly. They said at the agency, "You'll like it, it's a very friendly office. It's not like advertising or anything, it's only like politics, but it's very friendly." (*She moves to go*)

Terry Wait a moment, Shireen. Where were we?

Kent Why not?

Terry Why not what?

Kent Why can't I go on the switch?

Terry (*calmly*) Hold on, Kent. Let's just get this other business sorted out first. Now, Jacqui ...

Jacqui is studying the magazine that Terry looked at earlier

Jacqui (*to Terry, holding the magazine*) Rather appropriate, my sweet. He's having her across the desk.

Terry Now come on, love ...

Jacqui I wonder why you did it on *my* desk instead of yours. I wonder if you know yourself. There's something very twisted hidden away there.

Terry I don't think I know what you're talking about.

Hilary (*quietly*) Well, we *do* know what she's talking about. And it's true.

Terry Hilary ...

Hilary No, but if we believe in openness ...

Jacqui (*to Terry*) I think you've found a real disciple here.

Jacqui puts all the bits and pieces out of her drawer into her handbag

Hilary (*to Terry*) You and Jacqui, for instance. I think we should be told clearly what the arrangement is between you two, so we all know where we stand.

Jacqui Oh, don't worry about *me*, my precious.

Hilary (*to Jacqui*) No, we *all* need to know. All of us. (*To Terry*) And about the arrangement between you and me.

Terry Right. OK. Now ...

Hilary It's a difficult situation for me to accept. It's probably an even more
difficult one for her. But if we know what it is then we can at least try. (*She
looks at the floor*)

Jacqui goes out of the corridor door

I know it's not easy to talk about this. It's not easy for any of us. But it's
what you said, that first evening. You said we were making a city where
all the houses had walls of golden glass. Transparent gold.

Jacqui comes back with her overcoat

Inside the houses people were living all kinds of different lives, with all
kinds of different arrangements amongst themselves. Some very *comic*
arrangements — that's what you said. But nothing hidden. Everything
visible.

Jacqui This is the Book of Revelation? Yes, I've heard all the Revelation bit,
all the heaven bit. So why don't you do it in front of us all? On the desk.
Now. Why not? It's not quite high enough for comfort, I know that from
my own experience. Though I have to admit that was some years ago. You
could perch yourself up on the files again, the way you did before. Or how
about using the accounts? They're all yours now. (*She throws all the
paperwork that she had in her drawer down in front of Hilary*)

Terry (*to Jacqui*) Let's talk about this, shall we, before we do anything too
hasty ...

Jacqui (*to Hilary*) You want to know why I gave you a job here? Because
I thought you were a kind of daughter. You want to know what he's going
to be thinking when he's got you sitting up on the accounts? The same.

Pause. Hilary glances at Terry, then she looks back at the floor

Terry Jacqui, my love ...

Jacqui What do you feel about all this, Liz? Shireen, how about you? Let's
all talk about it. Or Kent. Yes, what are *your* feelings about all this, Kent,
my sweet?

Kent (*shrugging*) Go on the switch.

Pause. Terry's temper suddenly goes. He slams the file down on the desk

Terry No! I told you! No! Got that? No!

Pause

Hilary Anyway ...

Terry (*to Kent*) You want to know why not? All right, Kent, I'll tell you why not. Because you haven't got the brains. See? Because you haven't got the style. Right? So you'll just have to go back in the mailroom with Kevin. And don't tell me you don't want to work with Kevin. Tell *him* — tell Kevin what's wrong with him. Kevin ... !

Terry jumps up and runs out to the mailroom

Liz Oh no! Not Kevin!
Jacqui Why not? Bring everyone down.
Shireen It was so nice in here! It was so friendly!

Terry comes back, dragging Kevin, knocking envelopes out of his hands, banging him into doors and furniture

Terry In here, Kevin! Nothing hidden? Right! Nothing hidden, then! So. Kent don't want to work with you no more, Kevin. Go on, Kent — why don't you want to work with him no more? Tell him!

Terry shakes Kevin about in front of Kent, who shrugs and shuffles

Hilary I don't see how this is going to help.
Terry (*to Hilary*) Oh, don't you? So that's *your* nerve gone! (*To Kent*) Tell him!
Jacqui No, but it's pathetic, taking it out on Kevin!
Terry (*to Jacqui*) And there goes yours! (*To Kent*) Tell him! (*To Jacqui*) And I'm not taking it out on Kevin, I'm taking it out on Kent, I'm taking it out on all of you, cause you got to listen to it. (*To Kent*) Tell him!

Kent shrugs

OK, Kevin, I'll tell you why Kent don't want to work with you. He don't want to work with you because he don't like you. He don't like you because you can't talk properly and you can't walk properly and you can't do your proper share of the work. And he don't like being lumped together with you cause that means we think he's just as useless as what you are. And he's right — that *is* what we think. OK, Kevin? OK, Kent?

Terry lets go of Kevin. He begins to simmer down

OK, Jacqui? OK, Hilary?

Hilary sits down in her chair, silenced. Jacqui buttons her coat

Jacqui (*to Hilary*) At least you'll get the newsletter properly spelled. You have to keep writing to all the branch secretaries. They'll never send you anything otherwise.

Terry Right, that's it, folks — the show's over. Anyone who's going — go. Anyone who's staying — back to work. (*To Kent*) You're going, are you? Coat? I'll get it for you. What about you, Kevin? Staying? Going?

Kevin Staying, staying.

Terry Back in there, then.

He bundles Kevin out into the corridor

Kevin goes back to the mailroom

(*To Liz*) And you. You got work to do.

Liz retreats into the library. Terry returns from the corridor with Kent's coat

Right. Out. P45? In the post.

He bundles Kent unceremoniously out of the main door

Shireen Terry, can I just say like, well ...

Terry No. Out. (*He holds the door open for her*)

Shireen goes

Jacqui collects up her things

People take what you say, they twist it round, and then they throw it in your face. Six years it took to put all this little lot together. One morning to blow it all apart again.

Jacqui (*throwing down the key*) The key to the drawer. I expect someone's going to need it. (*To Terry*) I couldn't spell. But I did manage to make the books balance. Six years, and never a moment's trouble with the books.

Terry *You* don't have to go ...

Jacqui goes out

Hang on, love, hang on ...

Terry follows her out

Pause. Then Hilary collects up all the papers that Jacqui threw down in front of her

Liz emerges cautiously from the library

Liz Suddenly — crack! Like a thunderstorm. I just wanted to put my head under the covers.

Hilary As soon as we've got the lobby out of the way I'm going get started on these accounts ...

She turns over the pages of Jacqui's exercise book. Liz sits down in Jacqui's place, and tries to fit the drawer back into its slot

Liz (*laughing*) And you! You were so angry! You went a lovely deep red again, like the wallpaper in that Indian restaurant we went to!

The expression on Hilary's face makes her stop laughing. She puts the drawer down

Look, don't start feeling guilty! You were right to say all that! And it's a good thing she's gone — you know it is! She was useless. She just put everyone's back up ... Shireen and Kent would have gone anyway, sooner or later ... Listen, I expect now you'll have things to do next weekend ...

Hilary (*bleakly*) Will I?

Liz I mean, I assume ... well ... you know ...

Hilary I assume that this time he'll at any rate tell me.

Liz But if you *do* ever want someone to talk to ... Or somewhere to stay ...

Hilary Yes. Thank you ... These accounts. I suppose she was balancing them with her own money, was she? I suppose that was the great secret.

Liz (*shrugging*) I don't know. I've never thought about it.

Hilary looks at her in amazement

What?

Hilary You never wondered where the money came from?

Liz laughs

All the things in life we never wonder about.

Liz It'll be all right. Don't worry. I'll help with the books. We'll do them together! We'll manage somehow!

Hilary I don't think we will, actually. Not without Jacqui's money. I think we're finished.

Liz We've still got us. We've still got you and me!
Hilary And Kevin.

They turn to look. Behind the glass Kevin is standing wobbling on a chair, struggling with something on a high shelf. A mass of papers slips out of his hands and scatters

Liz And this! (*She holds up the file*)
Hilary Yes ... (*She takes it and looks at it thoughtfully*)
Liz What's he going to do with it?
Hilary You mean what are *we* going to do with it?
Liz Oh, I see. But if Terry won't ... ?
Hilary We'll do it ourselves.

Terry comes slowly in and stands saying nothing. The collar of his jacket is turned up against the cold, and he is slowly rubbing his hands together, not looking at them

Terry Sorry about all that. Either I should have been better than I was, or else I should have been worse. Excess of moderation, that's where I went wrong.
Hilary It was Jacqui's money, was it?
Terry I don't know.
Hilary You never asked?
Terry Who looks in the back of the clock, if the clock's going?
Hilary Yes, well I think our Hassam lobby tomorrow may be the last thing we do.
Terry Bad as that?
Hilary So ... (*She holds up the file*)
Terry What?
Hilary Get it copied. Hand it out. At the lobby.

Pause. Terry sits down in Jacqui's old place

Terry (*seriously*) Look, Hil ...
Hilary (*to Terry*) How many copies shall we do?
Terry OK, Hil, cut your own throat — I can't stop you. Put the knife in my hands — I won't do it, and that's that. The old fellow with his son in the Bible — yes. Me — no.
Hilary I know what she said. But you're *not* my father, and it's not your decision.
Terry Now come on, Hil. We got to be sensible about this.
Hilary (*holding the file*) Terry, they kicked him to death.

Terry They'll knock the life out of you, too, Hil.

Hilary Why does it matter about me, if it doesn't matter about him?

Terry Why? Same reason as it always is when something matters more than something else. Cause you're here and he's not. Cause you're close and he's distant. (*He picks up the drawer, and knocks the dust out of it*) Right. Back to work. (*He puts the drawer back into the desk*)

Hilary I don't accept that argument.

Terry You don't have to accept it.

Hilary But we do have to make a decision.

Terry I've made it.

He takes the file out of her hands, tosses it into the drawer, and slams the drawer shut. The phone begins to buzz

Moderation, Hil. Moderation. All right? (*Into the phone*) Hallo, OPEN. ... She's not here. She's gone home. You want the number? ... (*He goes into the switch*)

Liz (*to Hilary*) So?

Hilary So — ourselves.

Liz How?

Hilary glances at Terry, then takes the file out of the drawer

Hilary Same way as I did before.

Hilary takes the file into the mailroom

Terry emerges from the switch

Terry What's worse, Liz — when people won't do what you tell them, or when they do?

Liz glances towards the mailroom, where Hilary is setting to work at the copier

Liz I suppose we'll find out.

Terry We're not going to let her do it, are we, Liz? Don't want to put her away, do you?

Liz She's helping Kevin with the copier.

Terry (*abstracted*) Or maybe you wouldn't mind. Half of you would. But then there's another half of you underneath. Top half tidying the desk. Bottom half kicking the legs away. Bit of that in everyone, though.

Liz Even in her?

Terry follows her gaze towards the mailroom. They watch Hilary as she copies the file

Terry I don't know, Liz. You look in through the window. You think you know what's going on ...
Liz Transparent gold ...
Terry I told *you* about it once.
Liz Yes.
Terry No secret.
Liz Or do you wish you'd pulled down a few blinds?
Terry (*thinking*) I don't want to pull down the blinds, Liz ... No, maybe one. We all need to pull down one blind. One window covered over somewhere ... Anyway, something'll turn up, don't you worry.
Liz Will it?
Terry Always has, Liz, always has. I walk into this cafe. There's this nice lady. Just got her divorce, and half the shares in the family investment trust ... And off we go again.

Hilary comes out of the mailroom, carrying the copy she has made, and the file concealed beneath it

So let's get this place cleaned up. Kevin!

Terry fetches Kevin's coat and takes it to the mailroom

(*Off*) Here, put your coat on. Little job for you.

Hilary quietly shows Liz the copy she has made

Liz What are you going to do with it?

Hilary puts the file back in the drawer

Hilary Have we got an address for Terry's friend on BBC News?
Liz Mike Edwards?

Hilary takes the address book back to her place

Terry emerges from the mailroom, followed by Kevin

Terry Sorry about the aggro I was giving you earlier. Won't happen again.
Kevin No, I'm somewhat gratified that other people ... occasionally have to say difficult things.

Terry OK. Now I want you to get rid of this bag of filth out of here. (*He pulls out the rubbish bag in which Kent dumped Kevin's magazines*) So ...

He looks at Hilary. She is busy addressing an envelope. He glances at Liz, puts a finger to his lips, then quietly opens the drawer, takes the file out, shows it to Liz, and puts it into the rubbish bag

Off you go, then, Kev. Drop it on someone else's doorstep. And don't remember which doorstep it was.

Kevin goes towards the main door

Hilary Wait a moment, Kevin.

Kevin stops. She puts the copy she made into the envelope she has addressed

Terry No, something'll pop up from somewhere. Bound to. Feel it in my bones.

Hilary (*giving the envelope to Kevin*) Put this in the post, will you?

Kevin goes out of the main door with the envelope and the sack of rubbish

Liz gives a little laugh. Terry looks at her, and smiles, and puts a finger to his lips to warn her. She puts a hand over her mouth, to stop herself laughing, and glances at Hilary, who smiles

Terry Right, start all over again. Only this time ... (*He locks the drawer*) I'll keep the key.

CURTAIN

FURNITURE AND PROPERTY LIST

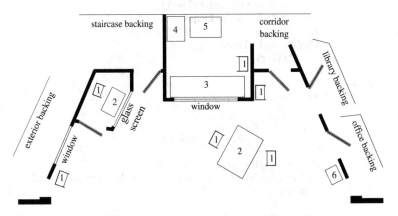

1 chairs   2 desks   3 table   4 photocopier   5 printer   6 small table

ACT I
SCENE 1

On stage: GENERAL OFFICE

Desk. *On it*: telephone, files, papers, pens, pencils, stapler, VDU and keyboard, shaded desk lamp (practical), box of tissues, large blue cloth bag containing barrister's wig. *In drawer*: child's painting, picture postcards, exercise book, spiral-bound shorthand book, papers. *Beside it*: **Jacqui**'s handbag, waste-paper basket with black bin-liner

5 chairs

Small table. *On it*: mugs, kettle, packet of slimbreads, jar of Nescafé, etc.

Doors to library and smaller office open

MAILROOM
Printer
Photocopier
Table. *On it*: envelopes
Chair
Waste-paper basket
Shelves. *On them*: stacks of paper, etc.

RECEPTION
Desk. *On it*: switchboard with headset
Chair

Off stage:	Coat (**Shireen**) Coat (**Liz**) Clean shirt on wire hanger (**Terry**) Socks and underwear (**Jacqui**) Dark suit (**Terry**) Clothes brush (**Terry**) Towel (**Terry**)
Personal:	**Roy**: wrist-watch **Shireen**: wrist-watch

SCENE 2

Set:	Post on reception desk Old, ex-army haversack, containing bar of chocolate and magazines, in mailroom
Re-set:	Items scattered about on desk top in general office
Off stage:	Bulky brown envelope containing file with photocopied pages (**Hilary**) Cardboard tray full of jam doughnuts (**Kent**)
Personal:	**Jacqui**: handbag containing various items **Terry**: money in pocket, bath-towel round neck **Hilary**: wrist-watch

ACT II
SCENE 1

Strike:	Broken mug Slimbreads from desk Brown envelope with file and photocopied pages Tray of doughnuts
Re-set:	Library door closed Items tidied on general office desk, with piles of files (some open) on both sides of desk
Set:	Newspapers in waste-paper basket beside general office desk Small table alongside desk

LIGHTING PLOT

Practical fittings required: desk lamp
Interior. The same scene throughout

ACT I, Scene 1. Night

To open: General interior lighting, practical on, night effect through window

Cue 1	**Terry** turns out the main lights	(Page 22)
	Snap off overhead lighting	
Cue 2	**Hilary** turns out the desk-light	(Page 22)
	Black-out	

ACT I, Scene 2. Day

To open: General interior lighting, daylight effect through window

No cues

ACT II, Scene 1. Night

To open: General interior lighting, night effect through window

No cues

ACT II, Scene 2. Day

To open: General interior lighting, daylight effect through window

No cues

Check: Wire coat-hanger hanging on door in general office

Off stage: Overcoat (**Shireen**)
                Overcoat (**Hilary**)
                File (**Terry**)
                Overcoat (**Jacqui**)
                Overcoat (**Liz**)

Personal: **Terry**: wrist-watch

ACT II
SCENE 2

Re-set: Files open on **Hilary**'s side of desk

Set: Two used cardboard plates under **Jacqui**'s side of desk

Off stage: Clean shirts on hangers (**Terry**)
                Jacqui's overcoat (**Terry**)
                Overcoat (**Shireen**)
                Typescript (**Roy**)
                Overcoat (**Jacqui**)
                Envelopes (**Kevin**)
                File, photocopy, large brown envelope (**Hilary**)
                Mail for posting (**Kevin**)

Personal: **Roy**: envelope in pocket

EFFECTS PLOT

ACT I

Cue 1   **Roy**: " 'Home Office. Secret.' "   (Page 1)
           Switchboard buzzes

Cue 2   **Terry**: goes out again   (Page 17)
           Sound of taps being turned on

Cue 3   **Terry**: "... in the stationery cupboard."   (Page 21)
           Switchboard buzzes softly

Cue 4   **Shireen**: "We're not supposed to know!"   (Page 26)
           Switchboard buzzes

ACT II

Cue 5   **Liz** opens the main door and listens   (Page 51)
           Sound of street door closing three flights below

Cue 6   **Shireen**: "It's so unfair!"   (Page 58)
           Switchboard buzzes

Cue 7   **Shireen**: "They spent the night in here!"   (Page 62)
           Switchboard buzzes

Cue 8   **Shireen**: " '... nothing ever happens in that office!' "   (Page 65)
           Switchboard buzzes

Cue 9   **Shireen**: "... ever since I came in this morning!" (Page 67)
           Switchboard buzzes; continue

Cue 10   **Kent** and **Shireen** straighten up   (Page 67)
           Buzzing stops

Cue 11   **Kent** shrugs   (Page 71)
           Switchboard buzzes; continue

Cue 12   **Terry** looks at the magazine   (Page 71)
           Buzzing stops

Cue 13   **Roy** begins to look through the file   (Page 73)
             Switchboard buzzes; continue

Cue 14   **Terry**: "Right. Cheers."   (Page 74)
             Buzzing stops

Cue 15   **Terry** slams the drawer shut   (Page 80)
             Switchboard buzzes